THE PONY DETECTIVES

Foxy:
Rivalry at Summer Camp

D0186131

First published in the UK in 2013 by Templar Publishing,

an imprint of The Templar Company Limited,

Deepdene Lodge, Deepdene Avenue, Dorking,

Surrey, RH5 4AT, UK

www.templarco.co.uk

Copyright © 2013 by Belinda Rapley

Cover design by Will Steele

Illustrations by Paul Nobbs, Dave Shephard and Debbie Clark

Cover photo by iStockphoto.com

First edition

All rights reserved

ISBN 978-1-84877-979-2

Printed and bound by CPI Group (UK) Ltd, Croydon, CR0 4YY

THE PONY DETECTIVES

Book Five

Foxy:
Rivalry at Summer Camp

by Belinda Rapley

templar

For Jake, welcome to the world

Rosie and Dancer

Mia and Wish

Alice and Scout

Charlie and Phantom

Chapter One

"DOVECOTE Hall!" Mia breathed, craning her neck to look out of the high, small window of Charlie's horsebox. The horsebox clunked down the gears, its engine whining. "We're here!"

Mia's three best friends, Alice, Rosie and Charlie, jumped onto the bench seat next to her, scattering buckets filled with horsey gear. From inside the horsebox they could see a rustic brick wall running alongside the lane. Beyond it there were rolling hills, dotted with cross-country fences. Charlie squeaked with excitement. The horsebox rumbled on along the lane, past ornate black iron gates, behind which stood a resplendent sandstone country house.

They heard the indicator tick-tocking and Charlie's dad took a left between two huge stone pillars. They slowly eased up a tree-lined avenue before turning into a large, dusty lorry park. It was already half full of horseboxes and trailers with their ramps down.

"I feel sick!" Alice gulped as their horsebox finally came to a halt. She curled her mousy brown hair behind her ears with slightly shaking fingers as she stared out of the window. Her nerves had started to take over and she looked panicky. "What if everyone's been to a hundred Pony Camps before? What if we get put into different teams? What if everyone else has got amazing ponies?"

"You've got an amazing pony, too, remember?" Mia reassured her, as Charlie opened the side door of the horsebox and they all jumped out.

Rosie shaded her eyes from the glaring sun as Mia slid her pink-framed sunglasses down. Charlie's dad helped them unbolt and lower the ramp at the back. Alice's bold grey pony, Scout, surveyed his new surroundings with bright eyes before jogging down the ramp. Dancer, Rosie's strawberry roan cob, followed, charging down like a bull. Rosie's loose haystack of blonde hair fell over her eyes at exactly the wrong moment, and she tripped, barrelling straight into Alice. Her friend giggled and grabbed Rosie's arm, keeping her upright. Mia led Wish Me Luck, dressed from head to toe in pink travelling gear, down next.

The three ponies waited near the bottom for Phantom, Charlie's sleek and striking thoroughbred. He stood quivering at the top for a moment, then launched himself down in one leap – Charlie, who was tall and willowy like her horse, only just managed to hang onto the lead rope. Hettie the sheep, Phantom's constant companion, trotted down last. Without Hettie, the black horse was nervy and anxious, but the sheep helped settle him. Hettie caused a few double-takes and "ooohs" from the girls and boys standing nearby as the four friends led their ponies under a shaded carriage arch.

The girls stepped back out into the sun and onto a big, grassy paddock. In front of them stood two rows of temporary stables, which faced each other. Each row had ten stables in it. The stables were constructed from metal frames with green canvas stretched tight to make the sides, back and front. There was a creamy white canvas roof covering it all, keeping the ponies inside cool.

"Right, who have we got here?" asked an instructor with cropped blonde hair and a name badge saying 'Melissa'. She breezed over and checked her list when they gave their names. "Okay, everyone's in teams of six. You four are in the purple team, along with two others, Holly and Amber. They're not here yet."

Alice exchanged a relieved look with her three best friends. She was never apart from the girls for any more than a day at a time. Not only did they all stable their ponies together at Blackberry Farm, they were also Pony Detectives, solving mysteries and cracking cases as a team. They had investigated five mysteries already, and were getting quite good at it, Alice thought proudly.

"You've got the four stables at the far end," Melissa said, "two on each side, nearest the tents in the campsite, okay?"

She handed out colour-coded name stickers.

"How lucky's that?" Mia smiled, as she placed her sticker on meticulously, making sure it was level. "Purple goes best with my pink top!"

Rosie stuck hers on upside down by mistake, making Alice and Charlie giggle.

Charlie led the way into the stables. Phantom spooked at every twitch from the green canvas. Wish stepped daintily over the grass, totally unfazed. Scout looked round, full of quiet curiosity, while behind him Dancer snorted dramatically, acting like she'd never seen another pony before.

Beyond the end of the stables Rosie could see four large orange tents neatly spaced in a horseshoe shape, with the tent doors opening into the middle. Each one had a tall pole beside it with a different coloured flag fluttering in the warm summer breeze.

Rosie put Dancer in the very end stable. Her stocky pony immediately scoured the floor with her muzzle, searching for anything edible. Once he was in, Scout swung round and rushed to the front of his stable, so that he could look out. Alice peered into the stable next door. There were shavings down, but it was empty.

"We'd better get the buckets so we can give our ponies a drink," Mia said, patting Wish. "They're probably thirsty after travelling in this heat."

As they headed back to the horsebox, boys and girls rushed past them in both directions.

Some of them looked a bit nervous, others were giggling and chatting already, forming little groups. There were four boys, who Charlie noticed were sticking closely together.

"I'll never remember who anyone is," Alice groaned, still feeling jittery, "there are so many people!"

The Pony Detectives grabbed their water buckets and quickly untied their haynets from the horsebox. As soon as they brought them to the stables, Dancer plunged her muzzle into the filled bucket, sloshing water around before drinking deeply. She raised her head and dribbled all over Rosie.

"Dancer!" Rosie squeaked.

Then they returned to the horsebox, gathered their tack and lugged it through the carriage arch. On either side of the archway were stone outbuildings. To the right there was a tack room and a room with all the mucking-out equipment. To the left, one storeroom was stacked with hay, and another was being used as the feed room.

There was a big whiteboard over the feed bins, with each pony's daily feeds written up neatly in black felt pen. There was one column for 'Medicines', with a note below advising, 'Instructors to administer'. Only two ponies had a tick in this column – Skylark and Topaz. *Magnesium Xtra* was written underneath the ticks in blue. The girls dropped their feed bags into their allocated bins, then rushed back out to get their own stuff to take to the tent. When it was all unloaded, they waved goodbye to Charlie's dad as he started up the engine and rolled out of Dovecote Hall.

The girls suddenly felt quite alone. They were walking under the archway back towards their tent when they heard running footsteps behind them.

"Hello! You've dropped something!"

The four friends turned round. A small girl

with honey-blonde hair jogged over to them, a rucksack slung over her shoulder with a whip poking out of it. She was gripping Rosie's copy of the latest *Pony Mad* magazine.

"Thanks. It must have fallen out of my bag," Rosie grinned.

"I'm surprised that nothing else escaped," Mia added, shaking her head at Rosie's overstuffed bag with its broken zip. "I'm Mia, by the way."

"Oh, hi," the girl said shyly, flushing pink. "I'm Holly."

"Holly? You're in our team!" Charlie beamed. "We're all purple!"

Holly smiled, looking relieved to have met some fellow campers. She turned the magazine over as she went to pass it back to Rosie, but froze in her tracks, suddenly captivated by the front cover photo. It was of a young woman riding a powerful chestnut horse over a massive ditch and brush fence. The rider had flowing auburn hair and was wearing lime-green cross-country silks. Her freckled, heart-shaped face was a picture of concentration.

"Are you a Lily Simpson fan?" Mia asked, nodding towards the rider on the cover.

"I think she's the best *ever*," Holly breathed, breaking out into a huge smile. "I'd love to be a top event rider one day, just like her."

It seemed like that summer the whole horsey community had gone Lily Simpson crazy, with every rider being inspired by her. The twenty-year-old had been born in the UK before moving to New Zealand with her family when she was three years old. She'd shot to fame after travelling back to the UK and winning the Badminton Horse Trials – a huge competition. Lily's dressage test on day one was faultless and on the next day her cross-country riding had been effortless and brave.

On the final day, her enormous horse, Firestorm, had still been full of energy and had bounced clear around the twisting show jumps. Lily had caused a stir – not to mention some jealousy among her fellow riders – after commentators and the press had hailed her as the most naturally gifted rider they'd ever seen.

Lily had loved the British competition circuit so much that she'd decided to stay. Her mum and younger sister had moved back to the UK with her, along with all their other horses, ponies and dogs. The next target on Lily and Firestorm's list was Burghley, one of the biggest three-day events of the year, and only a week away. If they won there, Lily would be the youngest ever rider to lift the trophy. Then she'd really shoot to superstardom in the horsey world.

Holly handed the magazine back to Rosie, and looked around anxiously. Alice realised that she wasn't the only one nervous about coming to camp, but at least she had her three best friends with her. It looked like Holly had arrived on her own. "Is your pony here already?"

Holly flushed again. "Um, no. I haven't got my own pony," she explained. "I've loaned one for this week from Hilltop Riding School. It's not far from here."

At that moment, a group of girls headed out of the stables and looked over at Holly and the Pony Detectives. One of them waved manically.

"Holly!"

"That's Watty," Holly said, making a bit of a face. "Well, it's Sarah Watson, really, but everyone calls her Watty. She's my next-door neighbour."

Watty rushed over to them, followed by five other girls. All of them were sporting blue-team badges. When the girls saw Rosie's copy of *Pony Mad*, they crowded round.

"Lily Simpson!" Watty exclaimed. "She lives just down the road! We're practically her neighbours, aren't we, Holly?"

Holly half smiled. "Well, kind of."

"She's been over in the UK for months now, looking for the right yard," Watty boomed. "She found a huge place with a farmhouse called Chestnut Grove at the start of the summer holidays. It's not far from here – it backs onto the Dovecote Hall estate."

"You're joking?" Charlie gasped, exchanging excited glances with her three friends.

The group had just opened *Pony Mad* to read the article about Lily when they were distracted by hoof beats. They turned to see a young man with an intense, brooding expression leading a grey pony with long, droopy ears towards them.

"Ah, Holly," the man said His glance dropped to the magazine for a moment, then he looked back up to the pony. "This is Skylark. He's going to be your loan pony for the week."

The pony had a thickset neck, a roman nose and hefty, round hooves. He gave a soft whicker as Holly approached him, his long ears pricking up. He looked hopeful of a treat.

"Thanks, Freddie," Holly said, stepping forward and patting her pony. Holly looked excited, but Alice saw her hands shake ever so slightly as she took hold of the rope.

"Do you want me to take your bag?" Alice asked. "I can put it in our tent if you like."

"Oh, thanks." Holly smiled gratefully, sliding it off her shoulder quickly and handing it to Alice. She turned and looked up at Skylark, then headed towards the stables with him marching beside her.

"Poor Holly." Watty sighed dramatically, looking round as if to invite questions.

"What's poor about her?" Rosie frowned.

"She's been lumped with Skylark for the week!" Watty explained in a whisper. "I learned to ride at Hilltop before my parents bought me my own pony, Ace, a few months ago. I sat on Skylark a couple of times and he *never* did a thing that I asked him to. He refused to canter and he ran out at every jump! In my opinion he's the worst pony Holly could have been loaned. I'm glad *I* haven't got him, that's for sure!"

Watty turned and disappeared towards the tack room, and the rest of the blue team followed her, giggling.

"I suspect that Watty's going to be rather full of opinions this week, don't you?" Rosie said, trying to ram her copy of *Pony Mad* into her bag. She gave up when the front cover ripped, and she began to read through the contents page instead.

"There's loads about Lily Simpson in here," she said, almost bumping into Alice as they walked to the stables.

"Look where you're going, Rosie," Alice giggled.

"I am," Rosie lied, her nose in the magazine. "Listen – there's a mini feature on her ponies and horses, including Firestorm and Foxy, her retired pony, and a bit about how she's preparing for Burghley too! Ooh, I'm going to read that right now. If I'm super professional from the start, like Lily Simpson, it might give me an edge in the competition this week!"

"Rosie, mind the—"

The next second Rosie went flying and landed in a heap on the grass, her bag tumbling beside her.

"...bucket!" Charlie giggled, as she and Alice hauled their friend upright again.

Rosie glared at the offending bucket.

"Oh, sorry, that's mine," Watty said, approaching from behind them. "I wondered where I'd left it..."

"Er, if you want to look super professional," Mia advised Rosie, "I think it might be better if you wait until we get to the tent to read your mag. Otherwise you'll be injured before you've even had a chance to put Lily's advice into practise!"

Chapter
Two

ROSIE charged over to their tent first, quickly unzipping the door and whipping back the flap. Inside there was one big space, with six camp beds lined up on the green groundsheet. A rucksack, with lots of badges from different countries stitched onto it, was laid on the camp bed in the far corner. But there was no sign of its owner. The other beds were empty and Rosie quickly flumped onto the nearest one. Alice put Holly's bag on the bed next to hers as Mia clicked open her pink suitcase and began to unpack her selection of purple jods and T-shirts but the others just dumped their bags.

"Come on, Mia," Charlie said impatiently. "I want to get back to the stables!"

"But my clothes will get seriously creased if I leave them all squashed on top of each other!" Mia tried to explain.

Rosie raised one eyebrow, questioningly.

"Okay then, I guess it can wait." Mia grinned, abandoned her unpacking, and followed the others back out into the sunshine.

They raced across the paddock, leaping into the shade of the covered stables to check how their ponies were. Phantom had retreated to the back corner of his stable, with Hettie by his front hooves. His head was high, the whites of his eyes showing slightly. Charlie smiled as she drew back the bolt and let herself in. When she first took Phantom on, she'd been scared of him and wary of his flashing teeth and stomping back hooves. Now she trusted her horse and her horse trusted her, and to Charlie, it was the best feeling in the world. She stepped quietly over to Phantom's head, and he lowered his muzzle, breathing warmly over her face. She breathed back into his nostrils and he flared them, taking in her scent, and then relaxed.

She found a treat in her pocket and waited while Phantom softly picked it from her hand. As he crunched it, she let herself out of the stable.

Rosie was trying to get Dancer's attention, but her mare was focused on one thing – guzzling her haynet. Alice went in to get a hug from Scout. She was still feeling a tiny bit nervous. Normally her reliable pony filled her with confidence, but this time Scout nudged Alice hard with his muzzle when she stroked him, as if he was a bit uncertain of his new surroundings too.

In the stable next to Mia's part-bred Arab, Wish, stood Holly's loan pony, Skylark. His large head was leaning over the stable door, nosily interested in everything and everyone who walked past. He gave a soft whicker as the girls gathered to say hello. Holly was in his stable, already grooming him.

"Is this your first camp?" Alice asked.

Holly nodded.

"Ours too."

Holly glanced down the stables. "I... I think everyone else has brought their own pony," she said, going pink again as she looked nervously at Alice. "Watty was sure I'd be the only rider here without my own."

"Well, Skylark's pretty much yours for the week, isn't he?" Rosie pointed out, thinking that Watty hadn't done much to make Holly feel better about the situation. "So that makes you exactly the same as the rest of us in my book."

"I guess so," Holly said, breaking into a smile. "I hadn't thought of it like that."

"And I don't actually own Scout," Alice said, as Holly leaned over the stable door. "He's on loan from the RSPCA."

"And I loan my horse, Phantom, too," Charlie added.

Holly's shoulders began to relax. "Thanks,"

she said, turning to hug the white pony who was nudging her with his strong muzzle, his large ears pricked. Skylark gave an almost silent whicker, looking hopeful, his nostrils fluttering.

"Have you ridden him before?" Alice asked, thinking of what Watty had said by the arch.

"No, never," Holly admitted. "I normally ride a pony called Jester on my weekly lesson at Hilltop. Freddie – the one who led Skylark here – his parents run Hilltop. He's just started teaching there, too. He watched my lesson last week so he could see which pony would be best for me to bring to camp. He thought I'd get along with Skylark."

Watty, who was eavesdropping as she walked past with a bucket of water for her pony, Ace, stopped for a second.

"Do you know why Freddie started teaching at Hilltop?" she asked, looking like she was bursting with gossip that she just had to share.

"Er, no…" Holly frowned.

Watty put down her bucket, looking at the four friends and Holly with an excited face. "He *used* to be in the British Junior Eventing team – he was awesomely talented, just like *Lily Simpson!*"

The girls gasped.

"So, he was tipped for the top and he'd just got his first proper horse who he was going to take to Burghley this year, where he'd have competed against Lily. But then he had a nasty fall over a fence and cracked some vertebrae in his spine! He was told if he fell off again he could be paralysed. He hasn't got on a horse since. His dreams of making it to the top were *shattered*."

"That's terrible!" Charlie grimaced.

Watty nodded. "His mum made him start teaching now that he can't compete any more. This is his first ever camp as an instructor. His mum knows Melissa, who's running the camp, really well. But I don't want Freddie as my team's instructor – I reckon he'll be super moody about being stuck here this week. And not just because of his accident."

"Why's that?" Mia asked.

"Because his girlfriend only happens to be Georgie Belle, Lily Simpson's biggest rival!" Watty revealed with a flourish. "Freddie's desperate for Georgie to do well at Burghley – she was being hailed as The Next Big Thing until Lily appeared on the scene and stole her thunder. But instead of going to support Georgie, Freddie has stay behind to teach us lot at camp!"

"How come you know so much about it?" Charlie asked.

"Because my sister's a weekend helper at Hilltop, that's how," Watty said smugly. "I get *all* the gossip!"

At the far end of the stables, a pony squealed indignantly as a bay cob was led past his door.

"I bet that's Ace being grumpy," Watty giggled. "I'd better go and check on him."

The stables grew steadily noisier as other ponies arrived and riders rushed back and forth between them and the tents. Alice smiled at a few other campers, who grinned back, saying "Hi".

A girl who introduced herself as Destiny wandered through the stables, checking everyone's badges. "Is anyone here in the red team?" she asked. "I can only find four of us – there should be two more!"

A couple of riders bobbed out from the middle stables and called over to Destiny. Then an eye-catching chestnut pony appeared at the far end of the walkway and grabbed everyone's attention, especially Skylark, who raised his head and whickered loudly, his big eyes bright and alert as he looked down to the end of the stables. The rider on top was as smart as her pony, dressed in a lime green T-shirt and beige jods. She had a heart-shaped, freckled face, pale green eyes and long auburn hair. She slid out of the expensive-looking saddle and gave her pony a pat.

Melissa, who was still busy meeting and greeting new campers, walked over to the girl. "Ah, our last-minute booking." She smiled. "You must be Amber. Amber Simpson? And I think your mum said over the phone that your pony's called Copper, is that right?"

As everyone – even the boys – began to nudge each other and a murmur rose in the stables, Amber nodded.

"Have you got your form? Your aunt said earlier when she dropped your stuff off that you'd be bringing it."

"Oh, yes, I've got it here," Amber said, in a strong New Zealand accent. She pulled out the Pony Camp form from her jodhpur pocket and handed it over to Melissa.

Charlie nudged her three friends. "Do you think that's Lily Simpson's sister?" she whispered. Rosie's eyes widened.

"You're in the purple team," Melissa said to Amber, and handed her a sticky label to put on her T-shirt. Rosie's eyes nearly popped out of her head.

Alice and Mia only just managed to not squeal out loud. Holly was still in with Skylark, but Alice knew she would be jumping up and down in excitement, as one of Lily Simpson's biggest fans. So, Alice got a big surprise when she saw Holly peek across at Amber, then quickly duck back inside Skylark's stable.

"Charlie and Rosie, could you show Amber where her stable is, and where your team's tent is? Thanks. Now, quiet everyone." Melissa tried to get everyone's attention amidst the excited whispering. "We've got an introductory talk in the dining hall this afternoon at one o'clock, where you'll get to meet the other instructors and find out more about the week ahead. Then there'll be lunch, followed by our welcome hack. Make sure you're ready in good time, please!"

As Melissa walked away into the sunshine, everyone suddenly broke into wild chatter and crowded round Amber, firing loads of questions at her.

"We were just talking about Lily earlier!" Emily, from the blue team, said. "We're all huge fans – and she's your sister! That's crazy! I'm so jealous!"

"Is she coming here this week?" Watty piped up. "Please say she is!"

Amber shook her head. "She left with Firestorm last night," she explained. "She headed to Burghley early to do some television stuff with Georgie Belle."

"That's Freddie's girlfriend," Watty butted in.

"Oh, right." Amber half smiled. "Well, the TV crew are doing a piece about their rivalry leading up to the big event."

"How come you haven't gone with Lily?" Watty demanded. "I'd have stowed away in the horsebox!"

"I guess Mum didn't want any distractions for Lily." Amber replied, and Alice noticed a slight edge to her voice. "My aunt's animal-sitting for us – Lily's been busy building her string of horses since we got over here, so we've got a bunch of youngsters, and a couple of our old favourites that we brought with us from New Zealand, as well as the dogs. Aunt Becca's lovely and everything, but she's a bit dippy, so Mum decided last-minute that it'd be better to pack me off here."

Everyone bunched up to watch her lead her pony into his stable. Copper's coat gleamed as it moved over his muscles, even in the shade. He arched his neck and his perfect mane hung neatly and evenly. He looked every inch a top competition pony. Scout leaned forward, reaching his nose round to sniff the new arrival, wondering what the fuss was about. Alice moved over to him and stroked his whiskery muzzle in case he was getting jealous. He lifted his nose and she kissed the end of it.

"I bet you're the most amazing rider," Watty gushed. "The rest of us might as well give up now. You'll ace the competition this week!"

"Well, I guess we'll just have to wait and see," Amber said breezily as she slid the saddle off, revealing a security identification freeze mark on Copper's back. A combination of letters and numbers stood out in white hairs from his bright chestnut coat.

"Let me take that saddle for you," Emily offered, rushing forward. She carried it carefully out to the tack room, like it was made of gold, then rushed back to get the bridle. Another girl from the blue team, whose label showed her name was Cat, grabbed the upturned green water bucket from the corner of the stable. She quickly filled it from the tap just outside the feed room. She walked as fast as she could back into the stable, like she didn't want to miss a second.

"He's a bit like a small Firestorm, isn't he?"

Watty asked, swinging on the open door. "They're the same colour chestnut."

"Chestnuts are all we have on the yard," Amber explained with a smile. "Lily's retired pony, Foxy, is chestnut and he took her to the top in Junior eventing. After that she said we should always stick to that colour for luck. It's kind of become our trademark now."

"Is that why you moved to Chestnut Grove?" Rosie asked.

Amber nodded. "Yup – how crazy's that?"

"Ooh, can I have your autograph?" one of the blue team girls asked, suddenly rummaging around in her pocket to find a piece of paper.

"Me?" Amber asked with a frown as she came out of Copper's stable and slid the bolt across.

"Well, you are kind of famous," Emily said. "Your sister's on the cover of this month's *Pony Mad*. Rosie's got a copy – I so wish I had one too!"

"Is that out already?" Amber asked, looking surprised.

Rosie nodded. "I haven't had a chance to read it yet though. It's stashed away in my tent, ready for bedtime!"

"Ooh, if I get a copy from the village, will you sign it?" Watty pleaded.

Suddenly there was a chorus of riders who wanted to rush out and buy *Pony Mad* to get them signed.

"Well, I'm not sure," Amber said, looking slightly awkward as she began to make her way with the crowd of campers towards Dovecote Hall.

Rosie looked behind just as they were leaving, and noticed that Holly was still in Skylark's stable. "Are you coming?" Rosie asked brightly. "It's almost time to meet in the dining hall."

"Um, I'll just finish this," Holly said, polishing Skylark's white coat with a stable rubber. "I'll catch up with you in a minute."

"Okay, see you in a bit," Rosie replied, with a smile. She jogged to catch up with her friends.

"I thought Holly was a huge Lily Simpson fan," Alice frowned. "But it's like she's barely noticed Amber's here."

"Maybe she's star-struck?" Charlie said as the friends rushed into the Hall through the huge back door.

The welcome cool of the stone-clad building hit them as they wiped their feet on the mat. They entered a large, echoey hallway, hung with big oil paintings in heavy, gilt frames. Signs pointed them to the dining room, which had two long wooden tables with benches on either side. Along one wall of the room a buffet was laid out, with jugs of juice, piles of sandwiches, cakes and fruit. Melissa stood with the other instructors at one end of the tables, smiling at everyone coming in.

Holly, carrying a book on pony care and

covered in Skylark's white hairs, crept in just as Melissa was about to start. She stole a glance at Amber, then sat down on her own near the other end of the bench.

"Okay, listen up everyone," Melissa called out, clapping her hands. "Before you start the buffet, I want to welcome you all to Pony Camp. I'll pin a timetable up for the week, over by the juices. As a general rule, you'll be expected to feed at seven thirty and be ready for your tack and turnout inspection by ten. Then there'll be a morning lesson in your teams. Lunch will be at twelve thirty, followed by a stable management demo and an afternoon lesson or fun ride at three. We've got a pool here, so in the evenings you can go swimming, and there'll be other fun stuff to get involved in, too. Oh, and there's one strict ground rule – no one is to leave the camp without permission. Okay?"

Everyone nodded, and murmured a "yes".

"Now, there'll also be team and individual competitions running throughout the week," Melissa continued.

Alice turned to look at Rosie, feeling nerves mixing with her excitement.

"Each day you'll be awarded marks out of ten from your instructor for your turnout, and then again for your riding. These points will accumulate throughout the week. I'll put the points up on a score sheet each morning at breakfast time. There'll be further points awarded in the cross-country event on Friday."

Next Melissa ran through which team had which instructor. She would be instructing the red team, Beth was taking the blues and Lara the green team. That left the purple team with Freddie. Rosie made a face, making Alice giggle.

"We'll go out all together for our welcome hack around the village as soon as lunch is over," Melissa announced, "so once the plates are cleared, make your way to the yard and I'll meet you, all tacked up and mounted, at two thirty sharp. I hope you all enjoy the week. Now, tuck in!"

Everyone rushed to the food. Then the whole camp crammed themselves as close to Amber as they could get. They talked over each other, asking endless questions – what was Lily *really* like? What was her favourite colour? Her favourite rider? Her star sign? Her favourite chocolate? Was she as pretty in real life as her pictures? Could they come and visit her at Chestnut Grove?

Amber sat there, hardly able to eat with answering all the questions. Suddenly her phone burst into life with a loud neigh. Amber's face lit up as she saw the screen. Everyone around her paused for a second. "You can ask Lily your questions yourselves if you want," she grinned. "This is her now."

The whole hall fell silent as Amber put Lily onto speakerphone.

"Hey, Lil, how's it going? Did you get to Burghley okay?"

Everyone tried not to giggle, and Watty clapped her hand over her own mouth.

"Amber, listen, I've just spoken to Aunt Becca," a voice rang out clearly. "She's crazy with worry – she can't find Foxy. He's disappeared from Chestnut Grove."

Chapter Three

AMBER froze as Lily carried on speaking, her panicked voice flooding out into the stunned hall.

"I'd forgotten to tell Aunt Becca about the supplement for Foxy's feed," Lily continued without waiting for a reply from her sister, "so I called her today about it. I said Foxy would be easy to pick out amongst the other horses and ponies. But then she phoned me back in a panic. She said she'd looked all over and there definitely wasn't a pony there with—"

Amber broke from her daze and quickly switched off the speakerphone, her fingers shaking. She pressed the phone to her ear, listened intently for a few moments, then spoke.

"So Foxy really *is* missing," Amber said in a small voice. Suddenly aware of everyone listening in, Amber hurried towards the door. "You can't come home because of this – you've *got* to stay and compete! I'll go home and help Aunt Becca look for him."

As she rushed out of the room, Watty started to flap, worried that their camp celebrity was about to make a dramatic exit before they'd even had a chance to see her ride. The murmuring in the hall grew as everyone speculated on what had happened. Everyone but Holly, Alice noticed, whose nose was buried in her book on pony care.

Mia turned to Charlie, Alice and Rosie. Her own excitement was reflected in her three friends' faces.

"If Foxy's missing," she whispered, "the Pony Detectives could help Lily and Amber look for him! From what Watty said earlier, the Simpsons don't live very far away."

"It could be our first celebrity case!" Rosie said, her eyes widening.

The past mysteries the Pony Detectives had solved included working out who stole a top showjumping pony, Moonlight. Then, when Alice faced losing her beloved Scout, they'd investigated a way to stop him being sold, securing his future with Alice for ever. Then they'd found the owners of a runaway pony *and* saved Phantom after his difficult behaviour nearly saw him sold once more. They were getting quite good at being detectives.

Amber walked back into the dining hall, her porcelain skin looking even paler than before. She sat down heavily next to the Pony Detectives, a deep frown etched into her forehead.

"What are you going to do?" Mia asked.

The rest of the camp crowded round, straining to hear.

"Lily doesn't know if Foxy's escaped, or... or if he's been taken deliberately," Amber said, sounding perplexed. Alice noticed Holly look up sharply from her book. She caught Alice's eye, flushed, then quickly glanced back at the page again. "She's called the police and the local rescue yards. She wanted to know if I saw anything out of the ordinary this morning, but I didn't."

"Was Foxy there when you left?" Alice asked.

Amber's cheeks reddened slightly.

"I... I don't know," she confessed. "I was in a bit of a rush, so I didn't get to check all the fields. He could have gone missing last night..."

"He might have just escaped from your yard," Charlie said, trying to make Amber feel better.

"That's true," Rosie agreed. "Firestorm's gone to Burghley, Copper's come here – maybe he tried to follow you? He could be wandering around somewhere nearby."

"Maybe," Amber said slowly. "I said I'd go home to help Aunt Becca look for him, but Mum and Lily won't hear of it. Lily's still thinking of coming back, but either way they're determined that this shouldn't spoil my week at camp."

It looked to Alice like the news about Foxy had already done that. "We've got our welcome hack this afternoon," Alice suggested. "Why don't we use it to ride round and search for Foxy then?"

Amber chewed her lip, looking uncertain.

"We can't lose anything by trying," Mia said, secretly wishing she'd come up with the idea. "If we split off into our teams, rather than hacking out together, we could cover lots of ground. Let's go and ask the instructors now."

The other Pony Detectives agreed and got up to leave, looking determined. Alice noticed that Amber hadn't moved. "Coming?" Alice asked.

Amber forced a smile and nodded, scraping back the bench as she stood up.

υ υ υ υ

Melissa was chatting with the other instructors in the lounge when the Pony Detectives raced in. When Mia explained in a rush about Foxy going missing, Melissa looked confused.

"Slow down a second," Melissa said. "Who's Foxy? That's not one of the ponies here, is it?"

"No," Freddie chipped in. "It's Lily's retired competition pony."

"That's the one," Mia said, looking across at Freddie. "He's gone missing from Chestnut Grove."

"Well, Chestnut Grove isn't far from here," Freddie pointed out. "Foxy could have wandered onto the Dovecote estate."

"We should definitely use the welcome hack to help with the search," Melissa said. "One of the teams should cover the grounds here, while the rest of us head out and search the local area."

Freddie grabbed a set of keys from the table.

"I can cover the grounds," he offered quickly. "I'll take the Land Rover and do it in no time."

"Okay, see you back here at four thirty, then," Melissa agreed, "ready to help everyone settle their ponies back into the stables."

They followed Freddie outside. As he roared off in his Land Rover, Melissa arranged for everyone to meet in the lorry park, then disappeared to get her own horse tacked up.

When the ponies were ready, everyone began to mount. Phantom pawed the ground, impatient to be off and Charlie had to keep him walking round slightly away from the ponies. Amber brought Copper out last and quietly jumped into the saddle. Alice noticed everyone craning their necks to get their first glimpse of the partnership in action.

As Melissa called for everyone to divide into their groups, Alice asked Amber for a description of Foxy.

"On the phone earlier," Mia added, "Lily mentioned that Foxy was easy to find among the rest of your ponies and horses at Chestnut Grove. Is he really distinctive?"

"No, not really," Amber said, as everyone fell silent to listen. "It's just that he's the only pony at the yard that Lily doesn't bother keeping neat, because he doesn't do much. She doesn't pull his mane or trim his tail any more, so they're quite bushy and his ears are a bit fluffy. He looks a bit roughed off. Um, apart from that, he's a fourteen-hand chestnut gelding."

Equipped with the description, the green team set off with Lara, closely followed by the blues, with Beth. Everyone could hear Watty giggling and shrieking on her way out of the drive.

"I bet she doesn't take this seriously at all," Mia tutted.

"Right, red team, you're with me," Melissa called out to the remaining riders. "And purple team, you're doubling up with us because Freddie doesn't ride."

As the red and purple teams started to move, Phantom snaked his head, his ears flattening. The next second Copper appeared at his shoulder and marched alongside him, tugging at the bit. Charlie glanced across at his anxious rider.

"Sorry," Amber said, shortening her reins, "he hates not being at the front."

They headed through the dappled shade of Dovecote Hall's tree-lined drive, and Melissa explained to those who knew the village which area they'd be covering.

"We've got Chestnut Grove on our patch," Charlie said, looking over at Amber. "Do you think we should start our search there?"

Amber shook her head. "There's no point. If he was near there, Aunt Becca would have found him by now. I think we should check out some of the less obvious places. The only trouble is I haven't lived around here long, and I don't know the area that well yet."

"I do," Holly called out gingerly from the back. She flushed pink as everyone turned to look at her. "I know pretty much every path around Chestnut Grove, and where they come out in the village."

ᘛ ᘛ ᘛ ᘛ

It turned out that Holly knew even more hidden tracks than Melissa, who then directed the big group alongside the estate wall, onto a tangle of bridleways and lanes. They rode past plenty of ponies grazing in fields but none of them matched Foxy's description, and there wasn't a lost-looking pony, wandering riderless, anywhere to be seen. They managed to fit in a few trots along some shaded wooded paths, and a canter up a long grassy slope. Phantom easily led, but Copper got competitive, matching him stride for stride and fighting against Amber for his head. Charlie noticed that Amber's face was stony and her knuckles were white as she gripped the reins. It seemed like Copper had picked up on Amber's anxious mood.

After an hour and a half of searching they'd drawn a blank and Melissa decided to call it a day. With hope failing, they began to head back to camp. They bumped into the green team as they turned onto a wide, rutted track, which ran through a sea of shimmering barley heads, swaying gently in the summer breeze.

"Did you see anything?" Mia asked the green team.

They shook their heads. "Nothing," one of them said. "You?"

"Not a single, roughed-off chestnut pony in sight," Rosie sighed.

"Well, at least we tried," Destiny from the red team said, leaning forward to pat her bay pony, Topaz.

At the end of the barley field they turned back onto a lane, and in another minute the estate walls came back into view.

As everyone gathered in the lorry park, Melissa thanked them all for looking, and asked them to get their ponies untacked, groomed and settled.

"Then it'll be time for their evening feed," she called out. "And while your dinner's cooking, feel free to have a dip in the pool."

The stables were bustling with everyone heading out to the tack room, grabbing skips to pick up droppings, grooming their ponies and refilling water buckets. Alice worked slowly, constantly distracted by Scout's little nudges or his big eyes following her round the stable. Scout lowered his head, blinking softly, and she kissed his eyebrow. By the time she'd sorted him out, the noise level from the stables had dropped in the stables and risen from the pool, and she could hear distant shrieks and splashes.

"Sounds like everyone's forgotten about Foxy already," Rosie said quietly, as she joined Alice, Mia and Charlie in Scout's stable.

"Not quite everyone," Mia pointed out, nodding further up the stables. Amber was leaning against Copper's half door, looking dejected as she fiddled with her phone. Suddenly a text message came through with a loud neigh, making the others jump. Amber quickly checked it and let out a long breath, as if she was relieved.

"Any news on Foxy?" Mia asked.

"No, but that was Lily," Amber explained. "She says she's really touched by everyone going out to look today. She's decided to stay and compete after all, rather than come back. She said that she's doing everything she can from where she is to find Foxy. She told me to at least try to relax and enjoy camp."

"Maybe a dip in the pool would help," Rosie suggested. Her hair was damp and stuck to her head after being squished into her hot hat. She couldn't wait to dive into the cool water.

"I guess it wouldn't hurt," Amber smiled.

"Are you coming, too?" Alice called over to Holly, who was fiddling about with Skylark's haynet.

"I've just got to get this up," Holly said, looking pink and frustrated as Skylark kept yanking great mouthfuls as she tried to tie the knot. As the others got to the stable, Holly finally managed it.

"Does that look okay?" she asked, avoiding Amber's eye.

Charlie popped in and checked it. "It just needs to be pulled up a bit higher, that's all," she explained, showing Holly how to adjust it.

"Thanks." She smiled sheepishly. "The ponies at Hilltop have their hay tipped into a hay rack, rather than tied up in a net. I've only seen it done in my pony care book."

Rosie heard another shriek from the pool

and felt even hotter and stickier. She hurried everyone back to the tent, then peeled off her jods and wriggled into her swimming costume under her sleeping bag. Finally she emerged, her towel wrapped round her. Amber started to sort through the stuff on her bed, and pulled her costume out of her bag. When they'd all changed, Holly grabbed her pony book, then they walked to the pool in the warm glow of the early evening sunshine.

"So, have you got any ideas what might have happened to Foxy?" Mia asked Amber.

Amber thought for a second. "Well, the only thing I can think is that one of the other top-ranked event riders is jealous," she suggested. "Lily's been getting so much attention recently. Maybe they took Foxy to ruin her chances of winning."

Rosie looked puzzled. "But Lily's riding Firestorm, not Foxy."

"I know, but even though Foxy's retired,

everyone on the eventing circuit knows how much he means to Lily," Amber explained. "She won't be able to perform anywhere near her best if she's worried that he's gone missing—"

Without warning, Amber's words choked in her throat.

"We don't have to give up yet," Mia said, trying to sound confident. "We'll still help you find Foxy."

Amber sighed. "What can any of us do while we're stuck here at camp? We've ridden around, and we didn't find him. Don't get me wrong – I'd love to keep looking, but if Foxy's been hidden somewhere outside this village, we don't stand a chance of finding him."

"Ah, but we're the Pony Detectives and we've helped find ponies before, even when their owners thought all hope was gone," Rosie continued proudly. "We're like a dog with a bone. We don't let go when a pony goes missing. Ever. Even if someone shakes that bone. Hard."

Alice nudged Rosie in the ribs, noticing Amber's confused expression.

"Is there anything else you can tell us about Foxy that might be helpful?" Alice asked.

"Is there a photo we could see?" Charlie chipped in.

"I don't just carry one round with me all the time, it's my sister's pony!" Amber said testily. The Pony Detectives glanced at each other. Amber caught their surprised looks, then she sighed. "Sorry, I didn't mean to snap. There might be a photo in *Pony Mad*. But listen, going on about Foxy all the time isn't going to help find him; it's just going to make me more upset, not less."

With that Amber put her towel down on one of the loungers around the sparkling pool and slipped into the water. Within seconds, Watty and rest of the blue team had swarmed round her. Holly quietly sat with her pony care book, glancing up occasionally.

"So, it sounds like this case is officially closed," Charlie said.

"*Officially*, maybe," Mia mused. "But *un*officially, I say we carry on trying to figure out what happened to Foxy. I know it's a long shot, but I don't think we should give up. After all, we haven't failed to solve a mystery yet. Agreed?"

"Agreed," Charlie, Rosie and Alice said in unison, grinning at each other.

"Maybe we should we get *Pony Mad* from the tent now," Mia suggested.

"If I have to walk all the way back to our tent or, for that matter, just stand here in this sun for another second I'm likely to spontaneously combust," Rosie said firmly. 'There's no way I can do any more investigating before I jump into this pool to cool down, and that's official."

"I guess we can leave it till later," Mia smiled.

Once that was settled, Rosie finally bombed into the water with a mega splash. Mia leaned away, squeaking as water flew towards her. Rosie bobbed back up, pushing her drenched haystack of blonde hair out of her eyes, her mind filled with thoughts of heroic detective work.

∪ ∪ ∪ ∪

After they'd fed their ponies, and eaten a dinner of chicken and corn-on-the-cob, cooked on a barbecue, everyone made up their ponies' breakfasts for the next day. They left them covered in the feed room, then headed to one of the sprawling reception rooms in the Hall. They sank into threadbare, squishy sofas and fat armchairs to watch some horsey DVDs.

When the last DVD had ended, Melissa popped her head round the door. "Right, time to get ready for bed," she said.

Everyone groaned good-naturedly. Destiny jumped up to turn off the television and the campers started to spill out into the sticky evening.

"Oooh, let's check on the ponies on the way to our tent!" Rosie grinned, rushing ahead. Dancer gave a soft whicker as Rosie reached the stables. A second later everyone piled in after her. Hettie was nibbling at the hay, and Phantom raised his head as Charlie appeared at his stable door. He snorted with a relaxed flutter of his nostrils. Scout rustled Alice for some treats and Dancer scraped her hoof, leaning against her door, worried she was missing out. Mia rubbed Wish's neck under her mane, making her stretch out her head blissfully.

After ten minutes, Melissa and Freddie came out, rounding everyone up and asking them to get washed and then go to their tents.

Rosie gave Dancer a final hug goodnight. The girls grabbed their wash bags and fought for space at the washroom sinks, before everyone finally raced to their tents. Mia brushed her thick, glossy hair while Holly quickly got changed into her pony print pyjamas and wriggled into her sleeping bag. Holly glanced around the tent before picking up her pony book to read. Then she pulled out a purple notebook and started to make notes.

"You're dedicated," Alice said, craning her neck to see properly.

Holly smiled. "I just want to make sure I do everything right for Skylark," she confessed.

Mia looked round. "We'll all help you," she said, "won't we?"

The others, including Amber, nodded.

Holly blushed furiously as Amber smiled back at her.

"I hope I do well and learn loads this week," Holly added, quietly. "My parents aren't horsey at all, and they're hoping that my obsession with ponies is just a passing phase. But I really want to show them it's more than that. They keep telling my Grammy to stop filling my head with horsey dreams. She used to work with horses, years ago. I think I must get my love of them from her."

Holly looked over at Amber and was about to say something more, when Amber started rummaging through her wash bag. Then Amber got up from her creaking camp bed.

"I must have left my toothbrush in the washroom," she explained. "I'd better pop out and get it."

She unzipped the door and headed into the fading light. Rosie glanced around her little patch in the tent. She shifted her sleeping bag and tipped up her pillow. With a frown, she started to delve into her stuffed bag.

"What's up?" Alice asked through a yawn, climbing onto her own bed.

"I can't find my copy of *Pony Mad*," Rosie said. She sifted through her clothes, throwing jods and T-shirts in every direction. Mia caught them and began sorting them into piles. "Has anyone seen it?"

Holly shook her head.

"Are you sure you brought it back into the tent after you fell over earlier?" Mia asked, using her torch to check the corners and under the camp beds in the increasing gloom.

"It was here," Rosie said, tipping out her bag over the green groundsheet.

"Well, it isn't now," Charlie said, helping her look.

"First Foxy, now this," Rosie frowned. "This is crime central!"

Mia was already in her matching pink shorts and T-shirt ready for bed. While Alice and Charlie quickly changed too, Mia climbed on top of her sleeping bag. "Well, nearly every Lily Simpson fan saw it earlier, and loads of them wanted a copy signed by Amber," she sighed. "So, half the camp knew which tent to find it in."

"But I can't believe anyone would be mean enough to take it," Rosie huffed. "I'd have let anyone borrow it, if they'd just asked."

Alice noticed Holly studying her book extra hard, although she hadn't turned a page for ages. Then she watched as Holly put it down and turned off her torch.

"Oh well," Rosie sighed, starting to bundle her stuff together and shove it near the foot of her sleeping bag in a haphazard pile. She found her cupcake-patterned pyjamas and wriggled into them. "I guess one article about Lily, Firestorm and Foxy was hardly going to help us solve the mystery of Foxy's disappearance, was it?"

The Pony Detectives lay in their pyjamas on top of their sleeping bags. Any lingering hope of tackling their first celebrity case was fading fast. They turned their torches off, but it still wasn't quite dark in the stuffy tent. After a few minutes of silence they heard footsteps running past their tent followed by squeals and giggles.

"I can recognise Watty's laugh already,"

70

Rosie smiled. The next second, Watty's head bobbed in. Her face dropped.

"Where's Amber?" she frowned, waving a bit of paper. "We've found something for her to sign!"

Behind Watty, Rosie could hear the rest of the blue team giggling.

"She nipped to the washroom," Charlie said, sitting up. "Although she's been ages. I hope she hasn't got lost."

At that moment Freddie's voice rang out. "That's enough talking," he said. "Time for sleep. And I want everyone back in their own tents, please!"

Watty giggled again and her face disappeared. The Pony Detectives settled back down onto their sleeping bags, just as Amber rushed in. She quickly got changed and slid into her sleeping bag.

"Did you find it?" Mia asked.

"What?" Amber frowned.

"Your toothbrush," Mia said.

"Oh, yes, thanks." Amber smiled, patting her wash bag.

The tent was silent for a few moments, and then there was a rustle.

"Does anyone fancy a midnight feast?" Rosie whispered.

Alice and Charlie began to giggle.

"Go to sleep, Rosie!" Mia said.

"Is that a no?" Rosie asked, as they all heard a sweet wrapper wrinkle. Alice glanced across, and could just about make out Holly smiling into the darkness. There was a small thud, as a sweet landed on Alice's sleeping bag. She saw another land on Holly's.

Alice lay in the heat, unwrapping the sweet. She had a feeling that camp was going to be packed full of fun.

Chapter Four

ROSIE woke in the green-tinted glow of the canvas after Mia prodded her for the fourth time. The early Sunday-morning sun was already starting to warm the tent.

"What time is it?" Rosie asked croakily, sitting up and rubbing her eyes.

"Time to get up," Charlie replied, pulling on her jodhpurs. "We've got inspections, remember?"

Rosie groaned. "Just five more minutes, please?"

"No, come on, we've got to feed the ponies," Alice said, nudging Rosie with her foot.

Rosie sat up and looked round. "Where are Holly and Amber?"

"Holly was out before we even woke up."

Charlie shrugged. "Amber left a few minutes ago."

Mia had already brushed and pulled back her long hair. She was dressed in a fresh pair of crease-free pink jods and a clean T-shirt. The others just grabbed what they'd had on the day before.

"I don't believe it," Rosie groaned, frantically rummaging through her untidy pile of clothes.

"What now?" Charlie asked, looking over.

"I can't find a single pair of socks!" Rosie explained. "I must've forgotten to pack them! If I go sockless all week my jodhpur boots will be really stinky!"

Alice giggled. "I've got some spare pairs. You can borrow them."

Charlie and Mia dug out a couple of spares, too. Rosie hastily pulled on a pair of Alice's, which were too tight and swapped them for Charlie's, which had a hole in, but Rosie kept them on anyway. While Mia tidied her corner of the tent, the others quickly raked brushes through their hair. Then they stepped out of the tent onto the dewy grass. A few of the other campers were starting to emerge too, and murmuring, sleepy voices having muffled conversations could be heard from other tents.

Holly was already busy forking a full barrow of muck onto the muck heap, but she joined the other teams as they made their way to the feed room.

"How long have you been up?" Charlie asked her as everyone collected their pony's feed bucket and brought them back to the stables.

"A while," Holly admitted as Skylark tucked into his feed. "I was too excited to sleep."

During morning stables, the blue team buzzed around Amber, helping to pick up Copper's droppings, or refill the water buckets. Once the mucking out was finished, everyone set about grooming their ponies, making them sparkle. The blue team insisted on fetching Copper's grooming kit and picking out his hooves for Amber.

After the camp had paused for breakfast, the riders headed back to the stables, grabbing their tack on the way. Scout's rack was next to Copper's, and as Alice gathered her gear, Watty and Emily rushed over. Watty quickly grabbed Copper's expensive saddle from the rack and Alice couldn't help but overhear her hushed conversation with Emily.

"Amber will *have* to invite us to Chestnut Grove after all this help, won't she?" Watty whispered, with a little giggle.

"Totally!" Emily grinned, unhooking the bridle.

They ran out, excited, to help tack up. Then stables were neatened, forelocks were combed and hooves were oiled. Watty and Emily fussed around Copper, and when Holly asked someone to check her tacking up before the inspection,

Amber volunteered in an instant, desperate to escape.

⌣ ⌣ ⌣ ⌣

As the sun rose in the cloudless sky, so too did the temperature. After the instructors inspected their team's stables, all the campers led their ponies over to four neatly kept, well-covered grass arenas. Freddie directed the purple team to the furthest one.

"Line up in the middle, please!" he called out.

The six riders stood next to their ponies. Skylark reached his large nose over towards Scout's, blowing gently down his nostrils. Scout blew back, making Alice and Holly smile as they watched their ponies make friends.

Freddie began inspecting each rider and pony. He pulled a long strand of hay from Dancer's tail. As he showed it to Rosie, Dancer made a dive for it. The girls all stifled a giggle.

"Remember, good riding," Freddie said sternly, "starts with good presentation."

"Ah, so *that's* where I've been going wrong," Rosie said, looking down at the juice stain on her T-shirt.

Freddie gave Wish, then Copper an appraising glance. "This is a very high standard of turnout," he said, as Mia and Amber exchanged a smile. "Make sure you both keep it up."

Then he pulled Charlie up for being scruffy compared to her beautifully presented horse, and Holly for missing a stable stain near Skylark's girth.

After the inspection was finished, Freddie helped everyone into the saddle, either legging them up or by holding stirrups and tightening girths.

"Before we start, I want to get an idea of everyone's aim for the week," he said, "and what everyone's ambition is in riding. Let's start with you, Alice."

78

"Um, I haven't ever ridden over a proper cross-country course before," Alice said, twiddling with Scout's mane. "So I want to learn how to get confident jumping big, solid fences."

Charlie said that her big ambition was to showjump Phantom at the Horse of the Year show, but at camp, she'd settle for having as much fun with him as possible. Rosie made everyone – except Freddie – laugh by saying that she'd just like Dancer to move less like a camel and more like a pony. Next up was Holly. She looked round a bit shyly, before clearing her throat.

"This might sound crazy," she said, avoiding looking at Amber, "but it's my dream to get to Burghley one day, just like Lily Simpson."

Alice noticed that the muscle in Freddie's jaw flickered for a second.

"A noble ambition," Freddie said, before taking a deep breath and turning to Mia.

Mia said that although she normally aimed for red rosettes in showing classes, this week she wanted her and Wish to try something new.

Freddie nodded and looked over at Amber. "And finally, Amber. What would you like to get out of this week?"

"Um, well, I'd like to compete at the highest level too," she said. "But my ambition right now is to come first in this week's competition."

Freddie nodded, then got the purple team going. He watched as they rode twenty-metre circles, figures of eight and serpentines in walk and trot. Charlie could feel Phantom was tense beneath the saddle, his ears pricked, looking for the slightest excuse to explode. She kept her reins as loose as she dared as she warmed her horse up, talking to him quietly under her breath. As she rode a half-circle, she saw Skylark on the track ahead of her, picking up his round hooves in a high-stepping walk. Charlie steered Phantom round him. On the other side of the arena, Scout was so excited that he squealed as he went into canter, setting Phantom off in a series of bucks. As Alice called across an apology, Rosie watched enviously.

"Why don't you ever get excited about schooling, Dancer?" she sighed. As if in response, Dancer trotted slower and slower until she finally ground to a shambling walk.

Wish was as unflappable as ever, even in the new surroundings. The palomino mare swished her cream tail, trotting and cantering elegantly around the arena, with Mia sitting neatly in the saddle. As she turned Wish onto a circle, Mia glanced across and saw Amber pushing Copper into an extended trot. Copper arched his neck, flicking his hooves flamboyantly.

"Watch out!" Alice squeaked.

Mia looked round at the last second, just as she was about to crash into Scout.

"Sorry!" Mia said, steering Wish quickly away.

"Concentrate, everyone," Freddie reminded them.

The group did as Freddie instructed, and Alice noticed that although Copper was the best schooled pony in the purple team, it was Skylark who really stood out. Alice knew that Holly hadn't been riding long, and so, she'd expected to see her riding like a novice. Instead, even though her position wasn't perfect and Freddie had to keep correcting her, she had a natural seat in the saddle. And it was clear from the way that Skylark's ears were flicking back and forward that he was already listening intently to this new rider. Holly was communicating to him so clearly that by the end of the lesson Skylark was responding to Holly's lightest command – first in trot, then in canter, too.

Eventually, Freddie called everyone into the middle of the arena. Copper stood square, and Amber sat tall on top, looking immaculate.

Freddie debriefed the ride, pointing out what he wanted them to improve on during the week. Holly had a long list, just like each of the Pony Detectives, but Freddie also singled her out for praise, saying that she had a light touch and that she'd already managed to form an impressive rapport with her pony. He left Amber until last, and Alice thought she looked slightly anxious as Freddie began his appraisal.

"Amber, Copper's clearly a beautifully schooled pony," he said, "and you ride very neatly."

Amber's pale face lit up, and a broad smile spread across her face.

"But don't forget that riding's not just about sitting in the saddle looking pretty," Freddie continued. "I want to see you tuning in to your pony and responding to what he's doing under you. That's what Holly did really well."

As Holly blushed at the praise, Amber's smile faded.

"I'll expect an improvement from all of you this afternoon," Freddie finished. "Now, time to get the ponies washed down."

♘ ♘ ♘ ♘

Once the ponies had all been taken back to the yard and hosed down, they were turned out into the paddocks beside the grass arenas. The instructors managed the grazing carefully. Electric ribbon was stretched between the post-and-rail fences to divide up the paddocks. Ponies that were stabled together at home were turned out together, while others, like Copper, had their own individual patches.

Each of the paddocks had some shade from the leafy canopy of horse chestnut trees dotted through them. The Pony Detectives turned their ponies out together, and Charlie ran back to lead Hettie to the field, too. Phantom paced restlessly, his head high, his fine mane swishing with each step until Hettie appeared at the gate and trotted over to him. Scout and Wish walked the perimeter of their new paddock, while Dancer found a shady spot and chomped great mouthfuls of grass like she'd been starved for years.

The only two that were on a strict 'no grass' diet and had to stay in the stables were Skylark and Destiny's pony, Topaz.

"How come they can't be turned out?" Rosie asked, chucking Dancer's headcollar and lead rope back into her stable. She thought how miserable Dancer would be if she couldn't stuff herself with grass.

"Topaz is prone to laminitis," Destiny explained as everyone rushed to the hall to grab packed lunches. "If she eats too much rich, sugary summer grass, it affects her hooves and can make her really lame."

"Freddie said that Skylark's exactly the same," Holly said, smiling at Destiny.

Suddenly Holly's face lit up. "I know! Why don't we take our sandwiches into the stables and eat them with Skylark and Topaz? That way they won't feel left out!"

Destiny agreed at once and they both ran off to keep their ponies company.

Rosie and the other Pony Detectives carried their lunches back outside into the sunshine and collapsed under the tree in their paddock. Amber came over and joined them.

"What do you all think of Freddie?" she asked. "I thought he was really picky."

Charlie was about to reply that she thought Freddie was pretty spot on when the blue team descended on their paddock. Amber groaned under her breath.

"We kept getting told off in our lesson," Watty giggled as she flumped down on the grass. "And it was all your fault, Amber!"

"Really? How come?" Amber frowned.

"Because we were gawping at your riding,

that's why!" Emily laughed. "We couldn't take our eyes off you and Copper! You looked a-ma-ZING!"

"Thanks!" Amber beamed, now looking genuinely pleased. For a while she soaked up all the admiration from the blue team, but she soon glazed over when Watty started rabbiting on about Lily again. Then, when Watty asked about Lily's favourite warm-up routines for Firestorm, Amber quickly made an excuse to disappear back to the tent. The blue team lost interest after their mini celebrity had disappeared, and they wandered back to check on their own ponies. The Pony Detectives headed to their tent, just as Holly was disappearing in through the door flap ahead of them. Amber was lying on her camp bed.

"Watty doesn't stop, does she?" Charlie said with a sympathetic smile, as Holly grabbed a packet of Polos from her bag.

Amber smiled back at Charlie. "I guess

that's a downfall of having a famous sister."

"She's exactly the same at school." Holly grimaced. "She drives our teachers mad too!"

Amber acted like she hadn't heard Holly, instead checking her watch.

"Right, time for stable management," Amber announced. "Are you all coming?"

Alice nodded, but she noticed that Amber had only looked at the four Pony Detectives. She glanced across to see if Holly had realised. The hurt look on Holly's face told Alice that she had.

ᘈ ᘈ ᘈ ᘈ

The afternoon demo was all about nutrition and feeding different kinds of ponies for different kinds of work. The teams sat together on the grass by the feed room, looking through all the sample feeds that the instructors handed round. Holly put her hand up and asked about laminitis, and

Freddie explained the causes and the symptoms.

"Laminitis is a painful disease which can, in some cases, be fatal," he said, as the teams listened intently. "There are different causes, like eating too much grass, or concussion. Blood flow is restricted to the sensitive tissues inside the hoof wall, which causes the tissues to swell and the hoof to become really sore. A pony will rock back on his heels to take the weight off the front of his hooves. It's much better to prevent laminitis than treat it, and that takes careful management."

Alice noticed Holly's face fall she listened to Freddie talk, and she wondered if her new friend was worrying about Skylark.

Next, Rosie asked which feed could give a pony more bounce, then the session ended with an activity where everyone had to work out how much food their ponies needed each day.

The afternoon riding lesson was flatwork again. Freddie made it his mission to wake

Dancer up and get her springing forward from the lightest command. Rosie worked so hard that by the end of the lesson she was complaining that her legs felt like jelly. But it was worth it – Dancer may have been disgruntled to begin with, but under Freddie's sharp gaze her step had become far more lively. Alice wasn't sure who was most surprised at the transformation: Dancer or Rosie.

Phantom produced some stunning work in between his excited outbursts. Copper had looked top class from the start, but Alice began to notice what Freddie was picking Amber up on. It was like Amber was just sitting on top of Copper, while Holly and Skylark were moving as one. The riding-school pony finished the lesson looking even more responsive than he had that morning. His neck was thick, but he arched it nicely, and his steps under Holly were deliberate and balanced.

As the purple team gathered round Freddie

at the end of the lesson, Rosie looked over at Skylark admiringly.

"He's so light on his hooves for a heavy pony," she puffed to Holly, wiping the sweat from her face. "The complete opposite of Dancer! You rode him brilliantly."

"Yes, you two definitely look like a winning combination," Freddie agreed, the first hint of a smile playing on his lips.

Holly flushed pink and jumped off, giving her hot, damp pony a hug. Alice noticed that, as Amber dismounted, her nose looked seriously put out of joint. They led their ponies in a group back to the hosepipe, where the rest of the camp had already gathered. Alice walked next to Amber, trying to think of ways to cheer her up.

"We've got our first jumping lesson tomorrow," Alice said, patting Scout's hot neck. "I bet that's Copper's speciality, isn't it? He looks really springy when you ride him."

Amber was about to reply but Watty was

eavesdropping and suddenly butted in.

"I so bet Lily's jumped massive fences! What do you reckon's the highest?"

The girls from the green and blue teams crowded round again to hear Amber's answers. They "ooohed" at each other as Amber told them about Lily jumping fences so big that she could stand under the top poles without her head touching them.

"Have you jumped that big too?" Emily gasped. Everyone stared at Amber.

"Well, not quite *that* big..." she said.

"How big then?" Emily insisted.

Amber held up her hand a bit uncertainly, at shoulder height. "About this."

As everyone gasped, Amber lowered her hand a tiny bit.

"Just think of the fences that Lily'll be jumping at Burghley," Charlie said, shaking her head. "She must be so brave. They look like the most massive, solid fences in the universe!"

"She does get a bit nervous," Amber said. "And she's definitely feeling the pressure more this week because of the whole thing in the media about her becoming the youngest rider to win."

"And that was before she had Foxy to worry about, too!" Watty added in.

Alice saw Amber wince, like she'd just been reminded of something she'd tried hard to forget.

Holly was standing in the sun, waiting quietly for her turn with the hose. Listening to the conversation, her face was anxious, like she had something on her mind. But then Skylark lifted his pink muzzle and rested it on Holly's shoulder. Holly broke into a huge smile as his big eyes closed sleepily, and she dropped a kiss on his whiskery muzzle.

"Those two have totally clicked," Charlie grinned as she scraped the excess water off Phantom. He danced away, crossly shaking his head as she squirted his mane and tail with fly spray. "It looks like they've known each other for years, not one day."

Next to her, Amber held onto Copper as she put sun cream on the end of his muzzle. "That's the difference between riding-school ponies and privately owned ones," she said, glancing over to where Holly was hosing down Skylark. The grey pony dropped his head to snuffle Holly's hair as she cooled his lower legs. "They're so docile, anyone can handle them really easily."

Alice picked up on the edge in Amber's voice. Holly had her back to them, but Alice saw her stiffen slightly, and she was sure she'd overheard.

Once the ponies had been fly-proofed, the girls turned them out in their paddocks. For the rest of the afternoon, everyone decided to collapse by the pool and laze in the baking sun.

"Are you coming?" Rosie asked Holly, as they headed back to the tent.

Holly hesitated, as if she was thinking about it, until she looked across at Amber and then seemed to change her mind. "Maybe not," she said, blushing. "I'll just read in the stables, I think."

She grabbed her book and wandered off on her own as the rest of the team made for the pool.

U U U U

As the orangey sun began to dip towards the treeline, everyone was still splashing about in the water or lounging on their towels.

Rosie checked her watch. "Snack time," she announced. "I'm like Dancer – I need feeding little and often."

She slid her flip-flops on and headed back to the tents. She walked through the stables, expecting to see Holly. Skylark's inquisitive face bobbed over his stable door and he whickered to Rosie. Holly wasn't there.

"Where's Holly, Skylark?" Rosie said, glancing round the empty stable. Rosie gave him a pat, then headed off to the tent. That was silent and empty too. Rosie found a cereal bar and was about to leave when she saw Holly's pony care book partly hidden under her pillow. Rosie frowned, then headed back to the pool.

"What's up?" Charlie asked, as she climbed out of the pool and saw Rosie's concerned expression.

"I can't see Holly anywhere," Rosie said, and explained about the book.

"Maybe she nipped into the Hall for something," Charlie suggested.

"We'd have seen her if she had," Mia said, sitting up.

But when it got to the ponies' feed time, there was still no sign of Holly.

The Pony Detectives wandered back from the pool. Behind them they heard a mobile phone neigh with an incoming text. They turned to each other and grinned, recognising Amber's message alert.

Amber was flanked by the blue team as she walked along, reading the text.

"Any update on Foxy?" Mia asked over her shoulder.

Amber looked up from her phone and shook her head. "Nope, no news yet," she said, "but Lily said that Firestorm's settled really well, which is brilliant."

Watty shrieked, and the blue team demanded to see the text for themselves. Mia turned back, leaving them to it, as Rosie, Alice and Charlie continued to talk about where Holly might be.

As they neared the tent, they saw the door flutter, like someone had just ducked through it. When they stepped in, Holly whipped round. She was puffing slightly, and had a sheen of perspiration over her face.

"Here you are!" Rosie exclaimed. "We wondered where you'd disappeared to. We were about to send out the search party."

Holly flushed and looked away. "I didn't disappear anywhere," she said. "I was here."

Rosie frowned. "Oh, right. Must've just missed you. Did you manage to read loads?"

"Erm, a bit," Holly replied, not quite looking at Rosie. But the pony care book was still tucked under her pillow, in exactly the same place Rosie had seen it over an hour earlier. Holly seemed distracted, and glanced over at Amber a couple of times. She took a deep breath, like she was steeling herself to speak. Then she braved it. "Um, Amber, there's something I wanted to tell you."

Amber yanked on her jodhpur boots without looking up. "Well, it's the ponies' feed time now," she said, slightly frostily. "Can't it wait?"

With that, Amber stalked out of the tent. Holly flushed again as the Pony Detectives exchanging surprised looks.

"What's up with her?" Charlie frowned.

"I don't know." Holly shrugged awkwardly, looking like she wished she'd kept quiet.

"Well, it's her loss," Alice said, feeling bad for Holly. "Has she missed out on something exciting?"

"Oh, no, not really," Holly replied quietly. "It wasn't that important."

As Holly turned to follow Amber out of the tent, Rosie noticed something odd on Holly's pale blue T-shirt.

"You're *covered* in chestnut pony hairs!" She grinned. "How did you manage that when Skylark's grey?"

Holly glanced down at her shoulder and

hastily brushed at them.

"I must've leaned against one of the other ponies," she mumbled. "Anyway, I'm off to the feed room. Coming?"

Holly dashed out of the tent, leaving the Pony Detectives even more puzzled than before.

"What was all that about?" Alice asked.

"I don't know," Mia frowned, "but one thing's for sure – Holly wasn't giving anything away about where she'd disappeared to this afternoon."

Chapter Five

MELISSA pinned the first score sheet up in the dining hall on Monday morning at breakfast time.

"I *said* you'd be in the lead!" Watty gushed to Amber as they crowded round.

"I wish I'd been able to watch you ride," one of the green team piped up. "Our arena was too far away to see!"

"We saw her and she was *brilliant*," Watty said. "Trust me!"

Amber looked slightly smug. "Funny, I thought Freddie said yesterday that Holly and Skylark were a winning combination. Maybe he was just being kind." She walked off to get her cereal.

Mia turned to check whether Holly had heard, but she was sitting down at the far end of the table with Alice. Mia looked back at the score sheet. She was in second place, with Destiny from the red team in third. Charlie and Alice were in mid-division with Holly, whose turnout score hadn't been great. Rosie was near the bottom just above Watty and Emily. Overall, the purple team were in second place, just behind the reds.

"I'm not sure that my scores will improve this morning," Rosie smiled, unfazed by her position. She sat down at the table, opposite Destiny. "Showjumping isn't exactly where Dancer's talents lie."

"Where *do* they lie then?" Destiny asked seriously.

"In eating," Rosie explained. "She's fab at that."

Destiny laughed and almost choked on her cereal, which set Rosie off too.

"Do you know what Skylark's like to jump?" Alice asked Holly at the other end of the table.

"No, I've never seen him jump anything at Hilltop," Holly said, "but his paces are pretty springy, so I reckon he'll be amazing... Well, I hope so anyway. I only started jumping at the beginning of this year, but I totally love it."

"I do too," Alice confessed, "but I'm a bit nervous about jumping in front of Amber."

Holly's face lit up. "Me too! I wonder if she'll be jumping massive fences... I hope Freddie doesn't make them too big today!"

Alice shivered. "Ugh, me neither!"

ʊ ʊ ʊ ʊ

Once the stables and the ponies had been inspected, the jumping lesson got underway. Freddie started them all off doing some grid work. He built up from three trotting poles on the ground to a cross pole, then two, then three fences in a row to get the ponies jumping athletically. They were streaming over the fences one after the other, so they didn't get much of a chance to watch each other. But then Freddie took away two fences and they started to ride one at a time over the single fence that remained.

"Let's have you first, Amber," Freddie called out across the grass arena.

The rest of the ride watched as Amber and Copper sailed over easily first time round. Freddie raised the fence, and this time Copper met it on the wrong stride and adjusted himself, taking off a bit early. Amber lost her balance momentarily and jagged the chestnut in the mouth. He raised his head in mid-air and clunked the pole with his back hoof. It bounced out of the cups, thudding to the ground.

"Copper was clever there," Freddie explained as Amber got Copper back under control and rode back to the group. "He sorted himself out, but because you used the reins to balance, rather than go with him, he knocked the pole. So, remember to let your reins slip a bit, or grab a handful of mane if your pony takes off unexpectedly. That way you don't hurt their mouths."

Phantom went next and he lit up the arena, clearing the fence by miles. Freddie raised the poles then sent Charlie round once more. As they finished, Freddie nodded, and called for the next rider. Scout followed and popped over the fences neatly, and Wish was hoof perfect. Then it was Rosie and Dancer's turn, and they crashed through the poles, demolishing the fence. Freddie yelled instructions at Rosie, and the next time, she managed to clamber over in canter before Freddie told them to rest.

Finally it was Holly's turn. Alice watched Holly as she approached with Skylark in a light, bouncy canter. She kept her eyes glued to the blue-and-white-striped poles as she turned

Skylark towards the jump. The pair met it on a perfect stride.

"Come round again, Holly," Freddie called out. He was watching her intensely, his head cocked to one side. Holly repeated the exercise. Once more the pair met the fence at just the right spot. Holly wasn't the neatest in the saddle, and she looked down, but she instinctively softened her hands and folded her upper body forward in harmony with Skylark.

Freddie made them jump one last time, raising the poles slightly. Without Holly appearing to do anything in the saddle, the pair met it on exactly the right stride again. Alice sat, amazed as she remembered Watty saying that Skylark was terrible at jumping. Holly was making it look easy.

"How do you manage to get Skylark to exactly the right take-off point *every* time?" Alice asked, thinking that she just hoped for the best and trusted Scout. "That's really hard!"

"It's probably just luck," Amber jumped in. She acted like she was joking, but Mia noticed that her smile didn't reach her eyes.

"Probably." Holly said modestly.

"There's nothing lucky about that," Freddie said firmly. "That's what you call natural talent."

Alice saw Amber's back stiffen, and she shot Holly a piercing glare.

"Okay, walk your ponies round to cool off properly," Freddie told them. "And remember to hose them down thoroughly before you turn them out."

As the ponies walked on a loose rein, Alice saw that Freddie's brooding gaze was fixed on Holly and Skylark – and so, too, was Amber's.

∪ ∪ ∪ ∪

When lunch was over the girls had a stable management lesson on bandaging legs for exercise, travelling and first aid. Rosie dropped her set of four exercise bandages on the way back from the tack room and spent most of the lesson picking hay strands off them and rolling them back up again.

Afterwards, all the teams joined together for a musical drill ride. The instructors made it fun, getting riders into pairs as they all rode round the arena, and calling out instructions to the music. At one point there were four pairs of riders performing a circle, with Rosie and Dancer in the middle, walking a ten-metre circle, while Charlie had to canter to keep in line with everyone on the outside of the circle.

As usual, Watty managed to create havoc. If she wasn't turning the wrong way, she was shrieking – especially during the exercise that required ponies to criss-cross each other at canter across the arena.

At the end of the drill ride, everyone rode back to the yard, grabbing headcollars and chucking down bridles. The ponies were led to the hosepipe and within seconds, foam from horse shampoo was flying in every direction.

Alice was careful to make sure none of the shampoo got into Scout's eyes. Once she'd finished washing him, she let Scout drink from the hosepipe. He nodded his head up and down, sploshing water everywhere. Alice glanced at her friends. "Did you see Amber's face when Holly got all the attention in that lesson?" she asked them quietly. Amber had finished fly-spraying Copper and had led him to the paddocks, but Alice didn't want anyone else to hear their conversation.

"Well, she'd better get used to it," Charlie pointed out, throwing a fly rug over Phantom, "because judging by Holly's skills in the saddle, I think there'll be a lot more where that came from."

When the ponies had been turned out, the boy campers decided to start a water fight. Mia stayed well clear in her neat outfit, but one of the boys, Harry, was an excellent shot and managed to soak every girl that ran past. Rosie squealed that she couldn't get her socks wet because she didn't have enough pairs left to change into. The air was filled with squeaks and shrieks as everyone tried to get near enough to get their revenge. In the end Charlie got nearest.

"Use a bucket! Here!" Rosie giggled, picking up Dancer's full one from her empty stable. Charlie grabbed it, and charged out of the stables at full pelt. She chucked it at the boys, just as they turned the hose on her.

Charlie squealed and the boys dodged out of the way, and the whole bucket whooshed straight into the muck heap.

"Loser!" Harry shouted, but as he came back to grab the hose again, he slipped on some wet droppings, and skidded into the muck heap.

All the girls watching from the safety of the stables fell into fits of laughter, until Harry began to throw handfuls of manure in all directions.

Suddenly Melissa appeared, drawn by the shrieks. "Right, that's enough," she said, trying to keep a straight face. "Harry, what *are* you doing in the muck heap?"

"Charlie chucked a bucket of water at me," Harry laughed.

"Only to get you back after you'd soaked everyone with the hose!" Charlie protested.

"But if you hadn't thrown the water," Harry pointed out, "I wouldn't have slipped into the muck heap!"

Melissa looked between them, pretending to be stern. "Well, Charlie, it looks like you're the lucky winner," she announced.

"Of what?" Charlie asked, suspiciously.

Melissa picked up a shavings fork and passed it to her. "You get to tidy up the muck heap!"

Charlie groaned and stomped over to it, giving Harry a little shove on the way past.

Mia, Rosie and Alice stayed behind to help Charlie as Melissa sent everyone else off to clean tack.

The four friends started to sweep the fallen, scattered droppings back. Then they dug into the front of the muck heap, piling it further back before starting to square off the edges.

Sweat made Rosie's eyes sting as she dug a bit further and hit something more solid. She tossed up another forkful but it didn't get very far, and quickly spilled back down again.

"What happened there?" Rosie frowned.

Mia peered at the muck heap. "There's something in there," she said, stepping forward. Forgetting her clean outfit for a second, she grabbed Rosie's fork and eased the muck-coated object out of the heap.

"It's *Pony Mad*!" Rosie said, surprised. Charlie, Alice and Mia gathered round.

"And look! I don't believe this! There's a rip in the cover – this is my copy!"

Rosie wiped her forehead, streaking it with muck at the same time. She picked up the magazine and shook some of the slimy, wet droppings off it.

Alice shook her head, totally confused. "But what on earth is your *Pony Mad* doing buried in the muck heap? I thought a Lily Simpson fan had taken it!"

"Me too," Mia said, "but at least this means we've finally got some more information on Foxy – and a photo!"

"I wouldn't be so sure about that," Rosie gulped.

"What are you talking about?" Charlie asked, leaning closer over her shoulder.

"Part of the Lily Simpson article's gone," Rosie said, looking up. "The competition preparation's still here, but the facts page about her other ponies, including Foxy, is missing."

"Why would anyone take just that bit?" Alice frowned.

The girls were silent for a second. Then they looked over to the other campers sitting around on hay bales, drying off in the sun and cleaning their tack. The green team's instructor, Lara, was standing nearby, checking their work and joking with them. But when the Pony Detectives saw Amber look over to where they were standing, they noticed that she wasn't smiling. In fact, she looked thoroughly fed up. She couldn't get near her own tack. The blue team had all argued over who was going to clean what of hers, and she'd been left with nothing.

"Something weird's going on here," Mia said. "I'm going to grab my notebook. We need to have a proper think about this."

While Mia rushed to the tent, the other three squelched to the hall to grab drinks. When they got to the open back door, Charlie suddenly held up her arm, and the others stopped. They could hear Freddie's lowered voice, talking in hushed tones just inside the hallway.

"Amber's really upset, too," they heard him whisper. Then he paused. "I know, but we've got to stick to the plan. You'll just have to trust me. I'll look after everything this end – you just concentrate on winning up there. Okay?"

Charlie stood, open-mouthed, as she stared at Rosie and Alice, who were straining to hear. She peeped round the doorway just as Freddie ended his phone call. The next second Melissa's voice rang out.

"Freddie, can you come in here a sec? We need to go through the list for the treasure hunt tomorrow."

Charlie saw Freddie jump and hastily drop his mobile on the side table as if it were on fire. Distracted, he disappeared into the lounge.

"Come on," Charlie said, pulling Alice and Rosie into the hallway. From just the other side of the lounge door they could hear the instructors chatting. Charlie sneaked closer to Freddie's phone. She peered at the swipe screen. It was still lit up – Freddie must have forgotten to lock it when he rushed off. Charlie looked back at her friends with a doubtful expression. "Should I?" she asked softly.

"You have to!" Rosie whispered dramatically. "Foxy will thank us if it helps us solve the case."

"*Just be quick!*" hissed Alice, nervously looking around her.

Charlie checked the phone to see who the last call had been made to, and a photograph of an eventer filled the screen.

"Georgie Belle…!" Rosie gasped.

Suddenly they heard footsteps coming towards them. The three girls turned on their heels, raced along the hallway and skidded breathlessly out of the back door.

Chapter
Six

HETTIE the sheep kept her distance, nibbling the grass around the roots of a tree while the ponies wandered over to see the girls. Even Phantom came near, huffing gently down his silky nostrils over Charlie. He ran his muzzle over her hair, then stepped lightly away to graze near Hettie. Charlie smiled. It wasn't that long ago that he'd hated to be in the same stable as Charlie. Now he was seeking her out in a big paddock, making her feel like the most special person alive.

The Pony Detectives sat down under the shade of the tree. Wish stood near them, sleepily whisking away the odd fly with her creamy tail, and nodding her head. After Scout and Dancer gave up rummaging the girls for treats, they stood head to tail, swatting flies and giving each other a lazy groom.

"So, let's look at what we've got," Mia said, opening her notebook at a clean page. At the top, she neatly wrote,

Lily Simpson's Missing Pony – Foxy

then continued, "Let's start with the facts."

"First off, it doesn't look like Foxy escaped from Chestnut Grove by himself," Charlie said, leaning against the thick, rough tree trunk. "He'd have turned up somewhere by now if he had."

"So that means that he must have been taken by someone deliberately," Alice concluded.

"Amber reckoned he was most likely taken by a rival," Rosie said.

"Someone at camp took *Pony Mad*," Mia

said as she wrote, "then hid it in the muck heap. But *only* after they'd ripped out part of the article that had a few facts about Foxy in it. Do you reckon there was something in that article they didn't want anyone to see?"

"Well, if that *is* the case," Alice said, starting to smile, "then someone here knows more about Foxy's disappearance than they're letting on."

"Yup, and we think we may have an idea now who that might be," Charlie said, feeling excited. Between them the girls relayed the conversation they'd just overheard to Mia.

"So, hang on," Mia said slowly, "Amber thought that a rival who wanted to ruin Lily's chances of success at Burghley might have stolen Foxy. But, if we've understood what you heard correctly, maybe Freddie's trying to scupper Lily's chances, leaving the path clear for his girlfriend, Georgie Belle, to win instead!"

"Freddie saw me with *Pony Mad*, too," Rosie added.

"And he's local, don't forget," Mia said, hastily scribbling. "So he must know the area like the back of his hand."

Charlie gasped. "Remember the hack on our first day? We all rode off to search the lanes and fields. But Freddie said immediately that he'd check out the estate."

"And if Freddie wanted to hide Foxy, it would have to be somewhere that he could easily keep an eye on him!" Rosie joined in. "Like right here! And, now he's supposedly checked the estate and said Foxy's not here, no one's likely to go poking around, are they?"

Charlie, Mia and Rosie grinned at each other.

"Now all we have to do is find where he's hidden Foxy, and that's it." Charlie smiled. "Our first celebrity case will be wrapped up!"

The girls stood up, stretching their aching legs. Scout walked purposefully over to them and the girls made a fuss of him, scratching his withers as he stretched out his neck, his upper lip wobbling in pleasure.

"So what do we do next?" Rosie asked.

"We've got the treasure hunt tomorrow afternoon," Mia said, checking a copy of the camp timetable she'd tucked into the front of her notebook. "And that's the perfect excuse to search every corner of the estate. If Foxy's here somewhere, the Pony Detectives will find him!"

Alice patted Scout, then the girls headed to the post-and-rail fencing, climbing over it on their way back to the stables.

"I never thought I'd say this," Charlie grinned, "but I actually can't wait to get our first session of cross-country over with tomorrow. Then we can get on with the treasure hunt! This time tomorrow, Foxy's mysterious disappearance may be solved!"

"And that might cheer Amber up at last," Mia said. "It doesn't seem like she's enjoying camp much…"

At breakfast on Tuesday morning, Amber stood staring at the updated score sheet pinned up above the cereals. She was still at the top, but her lead had decreased, and Holly had risen to joint third with Charlie. There were only twelve points in it. Mia was still ahead of them, because her turnout points were so high.

"Awesome, we're joint fourth!" Destiny beamed at Alice as she grabbed some toast. Alice grinned back. She'd risen a few places, but Dancer's jumping display hadn't earned Rosie many points. Yet, even with Rosie's score, the purple team had gone into first place, ahead of the reds by just three points. Watty and the blue team were still at the bottom, which she groaned about all through breakfast.

After they'd finished eating, everyone got ready for the ten o'clock inspection. Once they were tacked up, they rode onto the cross-country course at staggered times. That way there wasn't a huge bunch of riders all trying to jump the same fences. The purple and blue team stood together, watching the green and red teams head out. Destiny's pony Topaz was a handful, spinning and half rearing, but Destiny did well to sit to her and stay on while they warmed up.

Charlie circled Phantom as the morning grew hotter. He knew something different was happening and he'd started to sweat on his neck as he grew increasingly edgy, waiting for the off. Alice shifted uncomfortably in her tight body protector as she waited on board Scout, who was standing next to Skylark.

"I wish I was in your team," Watty groaned to Amber, "then I could watch you fly across all the huge fences and pretend I was watching Lily Simpson!"

Alice glanced sideways and noticed Amber grit her teeth, staying silent in her saddle.

But Emily carried on, unaware that Watty's

comment had made Amber bristle. "Copper looks like he was born to do cross-country," Emily added, admiring Copper's light frame.

"Unlike some *other* ponies," Watty said, nodding towards Holly's cobby pony. "Skylark's such a lump. I bet you wish Freddie had chosen a different pony for you this week, don't you, Holly?"

Mia, Alice and Rosie glared at Watty, but Charlie gave a small smile. She realised that Watty had no clue how to judge a good pony, even when one was standing right in front of her!

Holly looked flustered for a second. "I wouldn't swap Skylark for the world. My Grammy always says 'handsome is as handsome does'."

"Your Grammy can't have seen Skylark, then." Watty guffawed at her own joke, turning back to Emily who was snorting too. Beside them, Alice caught Amber making no effort to hide a smirk either.

Holly looked hurt as she reached forward to gently pull one of Skylark's big ears. The heavy pony turned his head, giving a soft whicker. Holly found him a Polo from her jodhpur pocket, which he lipped from her hand. He stood for a second with his face turned to her, like he was checking Holly was okay.

"Grammy says it's not about what a pony looks like on the outside," Holly continued in a quiet voice, "it's what's in their heart that counts. And I reckon Skylark's heart is huge."

At that moment Freddie called for the purple team to start warming up. Leaving Watty and the blue gang behind, he walked them over to the start of the cross-country course, carrying a long lunging whip with him. Then he got everyone riding in the cross-country position – short stirrups and raised out of their saddles. Alice felt her nerves tingle. But as Freddie talked them through the lesson ahead, he filled her with such confidence that she couldn't wait to send Scout over the first few inviting fences.

"Remember," Freddie called out, leaning on his long whip, "this should be fun for your pony, and for you. Right, let's jump!"

There were two different height options at each fence. Freddie said that anyone from his team could start over the lower options, then move up to the bigger height when they felt ready. Freddie sent Copper out first over the fences as the trailblazer. Amber immediately pointed her pony at the bigger of the two options. The rest of the ride watched in awe as he powered effortlessly across the grass and jumped quickly, barely breaking his stride over the solid fences. Amber didn't look like she was in charge, but her pony took good care of her, making all the decisions.

Alice followed Freddie's advice and started off over the smaller obstacles. She picked up canter and Scout flew over them bravely. Mia, not wanting Wish to get any knocks on the fences, jumped the smaller options at a steady canter. Holly did the same with Skylark. As Alice pulled Scout up, she turned to watch Holly. On the approach to the first fence, Skylark looked unsure, but Holly squeezed with her legs, her eyes fixed on the fence. She filled her pony with confidence and after just a moment's hesitation he soared over it.

"Good, Holly," Freddie called out, smiling as Holly proudly patted Skylark.

Rosie aimed for the lower option, too, then groaned as Dancer ground to a halt in front of the smallest log pile at fence one.

"She's so embarrassing," Rosie said, shamefaced.

"I've come prepared for Dancer today," Freddie announced, lifting the long whip. He waved it behind the strawberry roan cob on the approach next time round. Dancer's eyes goggled, Rosie grabbed a handful of mane and the pair launched over from canter. After the same approach at fences two and three – the tree trunk and the brush fence – something clicked in Rosie and she began to ride into the fences more firmly.

"Wow! Dancer's verging on energetic!" Rosie puffed, red-cheeked, as they regrouped after fence three.

Freddie then sent them out over the next three jumps – the hay rack, sloping rails and the stone wall. The ponies all flowed over them, one after the other, with Copper leading the ride once more. With each fence he was getting stronger and Amber was having difficulty holding him. He took off on the approach to each fence and jumped so enthusiastically that Amber was almost unseated at the sloping rails.

"You can always jump the smaller fences until you get your eye in," Freddie shouted, cupping his hand to his mouth. "Come round again, everyone."

But the second time round, Amber still stuck to the bigger options, ignoring Freddie's advice. As Copper sped up into the stone wall, he took off a stride early. Amber only just stayed on over the fence and landed back in the saddle with a thud. Copper flung up his head, ears back, charging forward until Amber yanked on the reins and finally got him back under control.

"Remember what I said yesterday," Freddie called out. "If your pony takes off early don't use his mouth for balance!"

Phantom showed his massive scope as he tackled the bullfinch. It had tall brush, which the ponies were meant to skip through, but the first time round Phantom cleared the full height of it, taking Charlie by surprise. She kept her balance – just – and slipped her reins, allowing Phantom his head.

"*Very* well ridden," Freddie said, patting Phantom. "Now take him round again at a faster canter so that he doesn't try to showjump it."

The second time round Phantom was hoof perfect as Charlie squeezed him and he picked up his speed, skimming through the top of the brush.

Next, Mia took Wish round sedately, despite Freddie trying to get her to move into a faster canter. Mia wanted Wish to have fun jumping, but she was still anxious about letting her go too fast in case she bashed the solid, fixed fences. If Wish picked up any knocks or bumps on her legs – even with tendon boots on – they might count against her in the show ring. There was no way Mia would let that happen.

Alice felt butterflies for a second as she turned Scout towards the bullfinch. Riding down to it, it looked ridiculously huge. Alice half closed her eyes in the last stride, but Scout could see through the tall, thin reeds and he jumped over the solid bottom section, brushing through the top. Alice felt the reeds knock against her painlessly before they landed safely on the other side.

"That was awesome!" Alice laughed. She turned in time to see Skylark jump. He was far springier than she'd expected and the expression on his face changed from one of surprise, to one of delight. As he landed he even squealed and put in a playful buck.

At the next fence, the hedge, Alice noticed that Freddie sent Holly out first. Skylark attacked the bigger hedge and Holly balanced easily on her pony. Holly was grinning in the air, and reached down to pat Skylark after they'd landed.

"I can't believe this is the first time she's ridden over cross-country fences," Rosie said, shaking her head. "I'll never be as good as she is today if I practice for a hundred years!"

"It's Skylark's first time too," Freddie added.

"They must *both* be naturals, then," Mia said, feeling pleased for Holly. "Don't you think?" she added, turning to Amber.

"Oh, I didn't see them jump," Amber said breezily as Holly rode back to the team. But Mia suspected that she had, because she looked like she'd just sucked on a seriously bitter lemon.

The rest of the team sailed over the hedge one by one. Amber kicked Copper into it hard, like she wanted him to put in an impressive jump so she could show off. Her pony responded, and put in an even more extravagant leap than Amber looked prepared for. She grabbed the front of the saddle and squeaked, losing a stirrup as Copper touched down on the other side.

"Right, that's it for this morning," Freddie said, as Amber rode back, pink-cheeked. "Give your ponies lots of praise and then get them washed down. The treasure hunt is at three o'clock this afternoon and it's timed, so don't be late!"

The Pony Detectives exchanged knowing glances. They'd need every second of the two-hour hunt, if they were going to find the treasure they were hunting for...

Chapter Seven

In the distance, the cross-country jumps shimmered in the afternoon heat. The four teams lined up alongside the paddocks, looking out over the rolling grassland of the estate. Melissa gave them a last-minute safety reminder to not gallop everywhere, and to remember to give their ponies lots of breaks because it was so hot. Then she blew a whistle and the teams cheered and set off in different directions at a canter.

Each team had been given a copy of a hand-drawn map of the campsite, a list of items to seek out, a saddle bag to put their finds in, and a pen. Amongst other things, the treasures included a pheasant feather, a pigeon feather, a smooth round stone, a plaiting band, an oak apple, a horseshoe and a purple wildflower. Each of the items on the list was worth a single point, except for one, which was worth twenty, but no one knew which.

The purple team trotted their ponies to the edge of the cross-country course. Then they pulled up by the alder trees that lined the brook.

"Do you think we should split up so we cover more ground?" Charlie asked, trying to get around the fact that she and her three friends were planning to go hunting for Foxy when they were meant to be searching for treasure with Amber and Holly.

"Um, okay," Amber agreed. "How should we do it?"

Alice suddenly realised what Charlie was getting at. She desperately wanted to stay with the rest of the Pony Detectives, but she also knew that there was no way Amber would agree to go off with Holly as a pair. "How about if me, Amber and Holly head off together?"

Mia gave Alice a grateful smile. "Sounds perfect."

"Why do we have to split *that* way?" Amber muttered moodily. "Why can't Holly go with Charlie's group rather than ours?"

Holly looked awkward for a second, fiddling with her glove.

"No, let's keep it like this," Mia said firmly, glaring at Amber. "Come on, we're wasting time just standing here."

They quickly divided the list in two and headed in different directions. When Charlie glanced behind her, she saw Amber moving Copper alongside Scout, pushing Holly and Skylark to the back of the small group.

Mia unfolded the map. "I can't see anywhere on here you could hide a pony. There isn't a single barn or separate paddock or anything."

"Well, this brook marks the boundary of the estate," Charlie said, peering over Mia's shoulder. "It starts just through these trees. I think we should follow it, so we can be completely sure there are no secret hideaways."

The girls picked up their reins and trotted along the tree line. To their left they could see the grassy slopes of the cross-country fences they'd jumped earlier. Charlie popped Phantom into canter. Mia and Rosie followed, trailing the meandering brook as it glistened and snaked its way around the edge of the estate.

They tried to stay in the shade of the trees, and brought their ponies back to walk now and again to give them a break in the heat. The cross-country fences swung away to the left and the brook disappeared out of sight. They kept going straight until the shouts and laughter from the other teams faded into the distance too.

"There's a pigeon feather in that bush," Charlie said, pointing. "We'd better pick it up. At least then we won't go back empty-handed."

"Good point," Rosie agreed, sliding from Dancer's saddle. She handed her reins to Mia.

"I'll see if I can find a smooth stone from the brook while I'm down here as well."

Rosie grabbed the feather, then ran through the trees and knelt down next to the brook. As she reached into the water for a stone, she looked over at the grassy bank opposite. There were some long scrape marks there, like a horse or pony had dithered on the far side before sliding down. Rosie squinted through the trees on the other side of the bank. Beyond them, there was no estate wall, and she could see a small, winding lane. On the other side of the lane stood a thick hedge, edged with post-and-rail fencing. Dipping her hand into the cold water, she grabbed a round, slimy stone and ran back to tell the others what she'd seen.

ひ ひ ひ ひ

"You'll never guess what!" Rosie gabbled. "It looks like a pony's been led from the lane out there, through the brook and onto the estate!"

She quickly dried off the stone on a tuft of grass, dropped it in the saddle bag, then jumped back onto Dancer.

"We'd better check that out," Charlie said impulsively. She immediately rode Phantom into the trees, towards the brook. "Are you coming?" she called over her shoulder to the others.

"But we're not meant to leave Dovecote Hall!" Mia squeaked.

"This is an emergency," Charlie replied firmly. "And we're here now – it'd be a shame to waste this chance to follow up on a lead. Come on!"

Rosie urged an indignant Dancer down the slope, through the brook and up the other side. Wish followed, picking her way neatly between the trees that led towards a narrow, winding lane. Right in front of them was a large hedge, which almost hid the paddocks beyond from view. Slightly further up the lane to their left stood a pale blue cottage with a thatched roof. An old lady was in the garden, pruning the flowers. She looked surprised at the sudden appearance of the ponies on the lane, and walked slowly to her front gate.

"Are you lost?" the old lady asked, looking at them slightly warily.

The three girls looked at each other for a moment, wondering how to explain what they were up to. Then Mia saw an opportunity.

"Kind of," she said, taking charge. "We're on a treasure hunt for our riding camp. We've just come from the Dovecote Hall estate. We're huge Lily Simpson fans though, so we thought we'd see if we could catch a glimpse of Chestnut Grove. Someone from camp lives there – we've been hearing all about it."

"Ah, yes, I know about the camp." The old lady relaxed and smiled warmly. She turned and gestured towards the high hedge beyond her small cottage garden. "Well, this paddock, next to my garden, is the furthest corner of Chestnut Grove. Not that it's used very often. The front entrance is quite a distance away – off a different lane entirely."

"Oh, right. Well, maybe we'll get to see that another day," Mia smiled, her heart rate rising. "Thanks!"

The old lady nodded, then watched as the girls turned their ponies. Mia, Rosie and Charlie couldn't keep the smiles from their faces as they headed through the trees and back across the brook onto the Dovecote estate.

"So, there are hoof prints in the brook right opposite the most remote corner of Chestnut Grove," Charlie said in a rush.

"Which means that Freddie could easily have led Foxy from his paddock," Mia figured, "across this brook, then hidden him in Dovecote Hall!"

"We'd better hurry up, then," Rosie said, starting to get excited. "We haven't got long to check out the rest of the estate and *find* Foxy!"

They trotted, then moved into canter, following the sweeping curve of the brook. Then, as they came around a gentle hill, they brought their ponies back to a walk. There, in front of them, was a large fenced paddock. To the side of it, right against the trees that edged the brook, stood three old barns.

"These aren't on the map," Rosie frowned, double-checking it.

"Making them the perfect place to hide a pony," Mia said triumphantly. Her heart began to beat faster as they walked over to them, their ponies' hooves thudding on the grass.

Mia jumped off Wish, and opened the gate for the others. She was just closing it when she gasped.

"What is it?" Charlie asked, turning round to look.

Mia plucked some hairs that had got stuck on the rough wooden gate post. They were thick

142

and long – clearly from a pony's tail. She held them up for the others to see. "Chestnut," she said, looking at Rosie and Charlie, wishing that Alice was with them to see their latest clues.

They walked their ponies towards the nearest barn with a mixture of fear and excitement. Mia slid the big, rusted bolt back on the huge doors and was about to yank it open when a horn beeped loudly behind them.

The three girls leaped out of their skins and Phantom shot across the field. Charlie just managed to stay in the saddle. As she reined him back around to rejoin her friends, she looked up to see a Land Rover bumping down the hill, from the direction of camp. It came to a bouncing halt by the barn, then Freddie jumped out.

"What are you looking for in there?" he snapped, frowning. Before he gave the girls a chance to answer, he continued. "I deliberately didn't put those barns on the map because they've got lots of equipment and machinery in them. They're not safe for anyone to go poking around in. Anyway, there are plenty of treasures nearer to camp. I suggest you start heading back there."

"But..." Charlie started. She couldn't believe they were having to leave the barns, especially as Freddie's reaction seemed to point even more strongly to something being hidden inside.

Mia gave Charlie a warning look. "Okay," she said. She swung back up into the saddle. They rode through the gate and Freddie clanked it shut behind them.

"Right, I'm going to carry on with my drive round to check on the rest of the teams," he said, as he started the engine. "I'll see you back at camp."

He waited until the three girls and their ponies had trotted up the small hill, away from the barns. Only then did he slowly pull away.

"Should we nip back?" Rosie asked.

Mia shook her head. "Freddie seemed determined that we should leave, so I reckon he might hang around, just to double check we don't head back. We can't risk it."

"So what do we do now?" Charlie asked, feeling frustrated.

"We go back tonight," Mia said, "when everyone's asleep."

"But it'll take ages to walk all this way," Rosie groaned.

"Well, then we only have one choice," Mia said. "We'll have to ride."

Chapter
Eight

"READY?" Charlie whispered. The others nodded. "Let's go."

Even after racing round for the last fifteen minutes of the treasure hunt, Charlie, Mia and Rosie had brought back a pitiful number of items from the list. Luckily Alice, Amber and Holly had done better, and the purple team managed to come second. Mia had updated Alice on their discoveries, then Alice had told them about the frosty atmosphere in her little treasure-hunt gang, with Amber criticising every idea Holly came up with.

After they'd untacked, the four friends had stashed their bridles in Wish's stable, rather than locking them in the tack room as usual.

After dinner and lights out, they hadn't undressed, just yanked their boots off, then hidden under their sleeping bags. It seemed like for ever before Holly and Amber fell asleep, especially as Amber had left her phone in the stables, and had disappeared off just before lights out to try and find it.

It was after midnight when Mia nudged the others, and the Pony Detectives finally crept out of the tent. An owl screeched from one of the paddocks and a deer barked an eerie call in the distance.

Alice jumped at every spooky sound, her breath shallow from fear of the dark, mixed with fear of being caught.

Just before they reached the stables, Alice noticed something small and white scrunched up into a ball in the grass. She bent down and picked it up, smoothed it out and then gasped, feeling the hairs on the back of her neck stand up.

"What is it?" Charlie whispered, pulling Alice inside the stables with the others. Skylark gave his customary welcome whicker. Charlie panicked and rushed over to pat him, in order to keep him quiet. For a second the girls stood still, their hearts thundering in the fresh silence, wondering if he'd woken anyone.

After a minute, they began to settle. Alice held out a crumpled white sachet with the words, 'Devil's Claw' typed on it. It was empty. Rosie whimpered, as Mia took the sachet and read the tiny wording on the back.

"This is a herbal remedy for horses," she frowned. "It says here it reduces swelling, and it gives pain relief too."

"The instructors are meant to dish out all the medication," Charlie pointed out. "Maybe one of them dropped the packet?"

"But why would they drop the packet out here, miles from the feed room?" Alice asked.

"And I'm pretty sure I didn't see devil's

claw written up on the feed board," Rosie said quietly. "It sounds terrifying – I'd definitely remember it!"

"Why don't we go and check quickly now?" Mia suggested. "It'll only take us five minutes."

As they were about to leave, Rosie noticed Dancer leaning against her stable door. The mare's eyes closely followed every move Rosie made. Rosie nipped over to her, and Dancer fluttered her nostrils, hopeful of a treat. "We'll be back in a second," Rosie whispered, "promise."

She quickly patted her pony, then the four girls left the stables and crept through the dark towards the feed room.

Charlie turned the big, old key in the feed-room door, which creaked open. It was cold and damp in there as they stepped in. The morning feeds were already made up and lined along the back wall. The girls looked through the gloom at the big whiteboard on the wall.

The only ponies with anything written in the medication column were Topaz and Skylark, for their laminitis.

"Nothing about devil's claw," Charlie said grimly. "So that means someone here is adding devil's claw to one of the ponies' feeds." Charlie frowned. "Without the instructors knowing."

"But why would anyone want to keep that secret?" Alice asked. At that moment, they heard Dancer bang impatiently on her stable door with her hoof.

"Quick," Rosie said, "Dancer must have heard the feed-room door open. I bet she thinks it's breakfast time. We'd better get going before she wakes up the whole camp. We haven't got time to solve this particular puzzle right now." She dashed out of the feed room and back towards the stables.

Mia shoved the mysterious sachet in her pocket as the Pony Detectives locked the feed room back up, then rushed to their ponies.

Next door to Scout, Copper lay asleep. His head wobbled sleepily as it rested on his front leg, his eyes closed. Alice stepped out as quietly as she could with Scout, trying not to wake him.

The sky was cloudless and a full moon illuminated the campsite. The four girls led their ponies quickly past the tents, holding their breath and hoping the ponies' hoof beats on the grass wouldn't wake the other campers. They checked the coast was clear, then they silently used the paddock fencing to slide onto their ponies' backs. Alice had ridden Scout bareback lots of times, but not as far as to the barns, and definitely not up and downhill. His summer coat was silken and warm and she could feel all his back muscles moving.

"I'm so glad that Dancer's got such a wide back," Rosie whispered. "She's so comfy." She glanced over to Charlie, who was sitting on the rangy and less well-padded Phantom. All the ponies seemed to think it was an adventure and they stepped out, their ears pricked as they made their way through the gloom.

They jogged quickly over the top of the hill, keen not to be making a silhouette for anyone at camp or in the Hall to see. Once out of sight on the other side, they slowed the pace again. Alice slipped slightly from side to side as Scout's hips rocked with the downward steps.

"There they are," Mia whispered, pointing through the trees. In the distance the three barns appeared, their tiled roofs clear in the moonlight. They trotted the rest of the way, then slid to the ground at the gate.

"I'll hold the ponies," Charlie offered. "I'd better stay out here with Phantom in case he does anything silly."

"I'll stay too," Rosie said. "There's no way you'd get me sniffing around inside those old wrecks – imagine the rats and creepy crawlies that could attack at any second."

"If it's all the same, Rosie," Alice said bleakly,

"I'd rather not imagine them."

An owl suddenly hooted right behind them, making them all leap out of their skins.

Alice passed Scout's reins to Rosie, and Charlie took Wish's. Then Alice and Mia crept up to the first barn – the one they'd tried to look in earlier. Mia shone her pocket torch through the slats. Inside it looked dusty, with broken shafts of moonbeams piercing the gloom. She could just make out a huge tractor towering monstrously in one corner. It wasn't the kind of place that a pony would be safe in, but even so, they had to check. They tiptoed to the doors, undid the bolt, then yanked the door. It opened with a loud groan that filled the still night air.

They stood together on the threshold, looking in. Mia swept the torch into the furthest dark corners. It smelled musty, with a strong whiff of oil. There was the huge tractor, with massive wheels that were taller than the girls, towering high off the ground. The rest was filled with farm clutter – a quad bike, spare wheels, rolls of chicken wire and odd bits of machinery.

"Come on," Mia whispered, regretting not changing out of her favourite pink jodhpurs, "we'd better go right in to check, just to be sure."

Alice could hear the waver in her friend's voice. Normally Mia was the brave one, but this time, without speaking, they linked arms to step over broken feed troughs and old tarpaulins. As they crept further in, they heard scuttling on the beams above them. Alice wanted to squeal at the thought of rats racing above her, or dropping on her hair. Instead, she and Mia sped up, hastily searching each corner before turning and gingerly hopping back into the night.

They closed the tall, gaping door and caught their breath. "One down," Mia said, sliding back the bolt. They moved onto the next barn – a smaller, brick-walled outbuilding with a tiled roof. It had an old, rusted padlock on the door. It looked like it hadn't been opened for years.

Mia shone the torch through a gap between the two doors, but it was piled up with junk.

"There's no way a pony could be hidden amongst that lot," Mia whispered.

"Last one, then," Alice gulped, as they stepped along to the third barn. It was bigger than the other two, and the door was closed, but not locked.

"Please be in here, Foxy," she whispered, almost under her breath, her heart thudding in her chest.

Together, the girls hauled the door open. They held their breath as they peered in, desperate to see a chestnut pony looking back at them from some dark corner. But instead the torch picked up a couple of old two-seater carriages and an ancient, cracked leather harness. Apart from that, the barn was empty.

Alice's heart dropped into her boots.

"Come on," Mia sighed, "we better tell the others there's no sign of him."

Rosie and Charlie were waiting for them. Phantom circled as Rosie and Charlie stood anxiously. Once they caught the look on Alice and Mia's faces, they both knew the result of the search without even having to ask.

"So what now?" Rosie said, feeling thoroughly disappointed by the unsuccessful night-time raid.

"Well, the clues definitely point to a pony being led into the estate through the brook, and we know that Chestnut Grove is just the other side of it," Charlie said, thinking hard. "And the chestnut hairs on that gate post prove that a chestnut pony's been through here recently. So, if Foxy isn't hidden in one of these barns, where else could he be?"

The girls looked round the field. In the opposite corner to the gate they'd come in through stood another gate. They led the ponies over to it. The other side of it was a dirt track, wide enough to drive down.

"Do you reckon we should check where that path leads?" Rosie asked, peering into the darkness unenthusiastically.

"Come on," Mia said, taking charge. "It'll be less scary if we all go."

She opened the gate and the girls tip-toed through, their ponies' hooves scrunching as they stepped off the grass onto the track. They edged their way down a dark path, jumping as the hawthorn hedges either side of them rustled. In the silence of the night, every tiny snap of a twig was magnified.

Rosie shivered, losing her nerve with each step. It didn't help that Dancer spooked and stepped on the back of her boot, almost knocking her over. Rosie's stumbling spooked Phantom and Scout too, unsettling the whole group. Her nerves now jangling, Rosie was about to suggest they turn back, when Mia stopped abruptly.

"Look!" she whispered.

The others followed Mia's gaze. They saw a bridleway leading off to the right, into woods. At the turning there was a metal sign, pointing into the darkness. On it, in peeling letters, was written: 'To Hilltop Riding School'.

"Freddie's parents run that riding school, don't they?" Alice gasped.

"Hang on," Charlie said, piecing everything together, "so Freddie might have led Foxy from Chestnut Grove, across the brook into the estate..."

"...but instead of hiding him somewhere *here*," Rosie continued, "he could have hidden him at Hilltop!"

"And guess what's on our timetable for tomorrow?" Mia smiled as they began to head back to the yard. "Our vaulting lesson – at Hilltop!"

"That'll give us the perfect opportunity to see if our theory's right," Alice said.

"And if it is," Charlie grinned, "we may *finally* find Foxy."

Chapter Nine

"YOU'LL never believe it, Amber!" Watty guffawed at breakfast on Wednesday morning as she stared up at the score sheet.

"Does she always have to be so loud?" Rosie groaned through a huge yawn. The Pony Detectives had put their ponies away the night before, then crept past Holly and Amber, climbed back into their sleeping bags, and crashed out straightaway. But Mia's alarm seemed to go off only minutes later. Now they all felt sluggish.

"What?" Amber asked, walking over to stand next to Watty.

"Holly's only gone and pinched the lead from you," Watty squawked, "on her riding-school slow-coach!"

Watty seemed to have been tickled by the scores, and was completely oblivious to the fact that Amber was quietly fuming beside her.

But it was clear that Holly had noticed. "It's only by a couple of points," she said, trying to play it down.

"I can count, you know," Amber snapped icily.

As she sat down at the long table, Rosie attempted to cheer her up, saying, "At least our team's still in first place."

But Amber just glowered at Rosie over her cereal.

ᘺ ᘺ ᘺ ᘺ

"Are we keeping you up?" Freddie asked as the Pony Detectives spent the warm-up yawning their heads off.

"Sorry," Charlie called back. Phantom skittered away from the first cross-country fence, sensing Charlie's lack of concentration, but they jumped it the next time round. Then the group moved on to the water complex. First there was a log pile, and then the ground sloped into a gulley of water with another slope back up on the other side. Two strides of canter would bring them to a narrow brush fence, called a skinny.

Everyone began by walking and trotting their ponies down the slope into the water and back up the other side before they tackled the log pile, water, and skinny fence together.

"Any volunteers to go first?" Freddie asked, looking round.

"I'll go," Amber offered, and pressed Copper into a strong canter.

"Short and bouncy, remember," Freddie called out, but Amber kicked on.

"Looks like she's going for top marks today," Charlie said, wincing as Copper stumbled slightly going into the water.

"I guess she wants to get back up to first place on the score sheet," Mia said, holding her breath as Amber sat still in the saddle.

Copper didn't see the skinny brush until the last second. He made a huge effort to twist over it, and Amber just managed to cling on.

"Amber, you've got a very honest pony there who wants to please, but you can't just sit there expecting Copper to do it *all* for you," Freddie called over. "You've got to *ride* as the fences get trickier."

Amber didn't look over, but jagged Copper in the mouth, looking frustrated. Freddie noticed and took a deep breath. "And don't tell your pony off. It wasn't his fault."

The rest of the riders followed. Dancer goggled and refused the skinny, but on the second attempt, with Rosie growling at her, she bundled over. Then they all moved on to the next fence, a trakehner.

"That looks hideous!" Rosie groaned as

they stared at a thick telegraph pole elevated diagonally across a shallow ditch.

Freddie talked through the approach, but there were still quite a few refusals, including a rare one from Wish. Mia's mare snorted and insisted on being allowed to inspect the ditch before she'd even think about jumping it. Once she'd seen it, she jumped it neatly enough.

Phantom ballooned over it, chucking Charlie so far out of the saddle that she flew off and landed on her feet next to him on the other side of the fence. She and Phantom both looked as surprised as each other. Freddie legged her back up and next time they stayed intact. By the third time, they jumped it perfectly.

Copper didn't bat an eyelid as he went over but Skylark had a good look at the trakehner, slowing on his approach. Holly kept her legs glued to his sides, and with a flicker of his ears, he ballooned over it. But, like Phantom, the next time round he was better, and soon Phantom,

Skylark and Copper were leading the other less confident ponies over the jump.

The copse came next. The ponies had to jump over some tyres, taking them from the sunshine into shady woods, ride downhill to a log pile at the bottom, then back up the other side of the hill and out into the sunshine over some more tyres. Alice sat back over the first fence as Scout jumped hesitantly. His hooves skidded down the hill before he scrambled over the log and flew up the hill the other side. He gave an excited buck after jumping back into the sunshine.

Holly sat back in her saddle. She steadied Skylark right up so that he popped into the shade slowly, earning a "well ridden" from Freddie. Phantom, on the other hand, nearly sky-rocketed Charlie when he launched over the first tyres not realising there was a drop the other side.

"Remember that your pony doesn't know what's coming next," Freddie called out to everyone as they rode to the next fence, "but *you* do. That's why you have to get the approach right so that they don't fly a drop fence, or go too slow for a big spread. And the approach is especially important for this next one."

Freddie walked over to the steps with them. There were three bounces up onto a level bank, then two strides followed by a drop down at the other end.

"You need to approach this fence with enough impulsion to get you to the top," Freddie explained, jumping up each step to demonstrate, "but at a very steady pace so you don't jump too big up the bounces. Has anyone ridden steps before?"

Amber's hand shot up.

"Um, okay, but maybe we should have Phantom or Skylark to go first," Freddie suggested hesitantly.

But Amber didn't listen. Instead, she trotted Copper in a sweeping circle, then picked up canter. She lined up for the first step.

"Steady him," Freddie called out. "You need to tell him to steady into this!"

But Amber kept on coming. Copper leaped up the first step with too much speed. He landed close to the next step but somehow managed to scramble up it. The honest gelding was about to stop, when Amber gave him a sharp tap with her whip on his shoulder. Copper flattened his ears and redoubled his efforts. He leaped up onto the top level in a tangle of legs, but was almost down on his nose and knees, with his rump higher than his head.

"Sit up!" Freddie yelled, but Amber was already halfway up Copper's neck as his momentum took him to the edge of the drop on the other side of the bank. He slammed the brakes on to avoid it. Amber was tipped over Copper's shoulder, and landed with a thud on the ground below.

Freddie rushed over to her, just as she stood

up and dusted herself down. Copper turned and popped back down the steps. He bumped into Wish and stopped, shaking. Mia leaned over and caught up his reins, scratching his withers to try and reassure him.

"I only fell off because my saddle was so slippery," Amber said. Mia could see the tears welling up in Amber's eyes as she took Copper's reins back. "Watty and her gang have been cleaning it every five seconds. If they'd left it alone I would have been fine!"

"You should be cleaning your own tack," Freddie pointed out, not unkindly.

"It's not like I don't *try*," Amber said, frustration making her voice waver, "they just won't leave my stuff alone."

Freddie nodded, then checked Copper. "He seems okay," Freddie said. "We were going to do the tiger trap last – but I think you should just pop Copper over something simple like the brush fence."

"But I'm fine to jump the tiger trap," Amber said, "honestly!"

"I'm thinking of Copper," Freddie said gently, "not just you."

Amber sighed, but she didn't argue any further. "I'll just take him back, then."

Freddie watched them walk away for a moment, then turned back to the others. "Right, let's see how the rest of you do."

As Holly and Skylark bobbed up the steps in a bouncy canter, Alice glanced behind her. Amber had stopped Copper and turned around to watch Holly jump.

U U U U

At lunch, Amber looked subdued. Watty and her gang had fussed round, asking if she'd hurt herself, carrying her lunch for her and not leaving her side for a second.

"I can't believe you fell off!" Watty said,

rubbing it in without meaning to, as all the camp headed back out of the Hall to eat outside. "Even *I* got up the steps in one piece!"

"You might get points for falling off with style, though," Emily giggled.

Amber smiled, but it looked to Alice like her teeth were gritted. When everyone started to separate into teams for the stable management lesson, Amber seemed relieved.

‿ ‿ ‿ ‿

Freddie talked to the purple team about good and bad conformation in a pony. He used Wish and Copper as examples of well-balanced conformation, pointing out their deep girths to house their lungs and heart, their short cannon bones and their strong backs.

"What about Dancer?" Rosie asked. "I'm sure she's an example of something. I'm just not quite sure what."

Dancer's eyes softened as Rosie rubbed her mare's nose affectionately.

Next Freddie ran through how to age a pony by looking at his teeth. The Pony Detectives and Holly spent the next ten minutes putting their fingers in Dancer's and Scout's mouths. They tried not to get their fingers crunched as they gently pulled back the patient ponies' lips to get a better look. Amber wandered off to check Copper's on her own.

When they were done, Freddie checked his watch.

"Right, your ponies have got a well-deserved break for the rest of the afternoon, but you all need to be ready in fifteen minutes," he said. "You'll be riding the specially trained vaulting ponies at Hilltop, so don't forget to bring your riding hats. And for those of you who want to go into the village afterwards, remember to bring some money with you for the shop."

The Pony Detectives exchanged an excited

glance, which didn't have much to do with the vaulting. They slid their ponies' headcollars off and walked back to the stables with their teams.

"Are you both going to the village afterwards?" Rosie asked Amber and Holly.

Amber shook her head and Holly shrugged.

"Um, I'm not sure yet," Holly said elusively. "I'm looking forward to seeing the ponies at Hilltop again, though."

She rushed off ahead, and the Pony Detectives hung back to talk.

"I wish we were going into the village first," Charlie said quietly. "If we don't get hold of a copy of *Pony Mad*, how are we supposed to even recognise Foxy?"

"We'll just have to memorise all the chestnuts at Hilltop," Rosie suggested. "Then we can compare them once we've bought a copy."

"We'd better get in there quick, though," Alice said. "Watty and her gang were all after copies too, remember?"

They hung up their headcollars, grabbed their damp riding hats and rushed to gather by the gates to walk to Hilltop Riding School. The blue team's instructor, Beth, was staying behind, but as they did a head count, they realised that one of the riders was missing, too.

"It's Amber," Holly said, looking round.

"We'll go and see where she is," Alice volunteered, dragging Rosie with her. They raced back through the stables, calling out to Skylark as he whickered to them, and out again to the tents. They flew through the tent door to find Amber sitting alone on her sleeping bag, her mobile phone next to her. She hastily wiped her eyes with the back of her hand before she looked up.

"I just called Mum," she said, trying to smile like nothing was wrong. "She didn't answer, though. She must be busy with Lily somewhere."

Alice felt bad for her. "Everyone's waiting

by the gate for you," she said. "We all wondered where you were."

"I've got a bit of a headache," Amber explained, "so I thought I'd stay behind. I might pop back and check on how Aunt Becca's doing at home instead, if Beth says that's okay."

Rosie was about to leave with Alice, when she suddenly thought of something. "If you do go home," she said, "could you find a photo of Foxy for us to see?"

Irritation flashed across Amber's face, just for a second. "If I remember," she muttered, before looking back down at her phone and lying back on her bed.

ひ ひ ひ ひ

"This is CRAZY!" Watty shrieked. She was kneeling on top of Monty, a chunky bay horse who was being lunged at walk in the outdoor school. She tightly gripped the surcingle, which

174

circled his girth with a loop by his withers, until her knuckles turned white. "I think I'm going to fall off!"

"Try concentrating, Sarah," Freddie called out from centre of the ring, smiling as Watty let out another yelp and almost slid off the pad on Monty's back. The rest of the camp was watching from the side of the ring, waiting excitedly for their turn and giggling at Watty's antics.

Holly watched for a bit, then sneaked off to say hello to some of the ponies. Mia watched as Holly leaned over the first stable door and gave a skewbald pony some fuss. Mia nudged her friends. "If we tag along with Holly," she whispered, "it gives us the perfect excuse to look round. And she'll know if any of the ponies are new."

Holly smiled when she saw them walking over.

"This is Patches, the very first pony I sat on," she said. The skewbald closed his eyes as Holly rubbed his ear.

"Do you know all the ponies here?" Alice asked, looking at the small, neat yard.

Holly nodded. "I'll show you round if you like," she said happily as she stepped to the next stable. "This is Bilbo – he's really naughty."

The four girls walked round the yard with Holly. There were a couple of chestnut ponies, but they both looked ancient and Holly said they'd been at the yard for ages. Finally they reached the last stable and any hope of finding Foxy at Hilltop disappeared at once.

"And this is Jester," Holly said, letting herself into the chunky dun pony's stable. She gave him an affectionate hug as he frisked her pockets and nudged her. "I always used to ride him – every Sunday since last summer."

"Is he your favourite?" Rosie asked.

Holly hesitated. "Um, kind of. At least, he was until this week. He taught me to canter and to jump, and he's really sweet. But now he's my joint favourite with Skylark."

At that moment Freddie's mum walked out of the office and joined them in the yard.

"Aha, did I hear Skylark's name?" she asked Holly, smiling at the girls. "How are you getting along with him, Holly?"

"I love him to pieces," Holly confessed, going slightly pink. "I'd have had fun on any pony, but Skylark's just so magical. He's what Grammy would call my once-in-a-lifetime pony, even though it's only for one week."

"I bet she'd love him too, and I'm so pleased you've clicked," Freddie's mum said, squeezing Holly's shoulder. "Freddie found Skylark for the school earlier this year. I'm still not convinced he's good riding-school material, but we'll just have to wait and see what the future holds for him."

Alice noticed Holly's crestfallen look, while Freddie's mum turned to the Pony Detectives. "And I hope you girls are getting a lot out of Freddie's teaching too?"

Rosie nodded. "He's been ace, especially considering that he'd rather have been at Burghley this week!"

"Whoever told you that?" Freddie's mum asked, laughing off the suggestion. Mia rolled her eyes at Rosie's lack of tact.

"Oh, I... I can't remember," Rosie mumbled.

"Well, they got it wrong," Freddie's mum smiled breezily. "It was Freddie's choice to stay for camp. He could have gone to Burghley, but he's passionate about teaching. He's been helping Georgie Belle, his girlfriend, with her training all summer, too."

Charlie had a sudden thought. "Does she keep her horses nearby, then?" she asked. "Has she got her own yard?"

"Oh, goodness, no. She's only got the one top horse at the moment," Freddie's mum explained. "She lives nearby, but she doesn't have her own land to keep her horse on, so she's always stabled him here. That's how she met Freddie.

Anyway, you better get back to your vaulting. Unless there was anything else you'd like to see?"

"Holly was just showing us your ponies," Mia said. "Have we seen them all?"

"This is it," Freddie's mum said, looking round. "It's not a big yard, but it suits us."

The girls thanked her and walked back to the school in time to see one of the boys stand up on Monty's back. He wobbled, his arms circling, but he managed to stay up without holding onto the surcingle for a whole turn of the school before sliding off and landing on his feet to a round of applause. As Holly rejoined the group by the side of the school waiting for their turn, Charlie turned to her three friends with a disappointed sigh.

"Is anyone else thinking what I'm thinking?" she asked.

Mia nodded. "If Foxy isn't anywhere at Dovecote Hall," she said quietly, "and he isn't being hidden here, then it can't have been Freddie that took Foxy, could it?"

"What about the phone call to Georgie, though?" Alice reminded Mia. "That was pretty suspicious."

"True," Mia agreed, "but I don't think that's enough on its own. Do you?"

Charlie shook her head. "I guess you're right."

"So that leaves us right back at square one," Rosie said, slumping against the fence.

"And we're running out of time," Alice added. "Today's Wednesday. We've only got a few days left at camp to find Foxy."

"Well, let's wait till we've got a copy of *Pony Mad*," Mia said, "and see if that gives us any inspiration."

ʊ ʊ ʊ ʊ

"What do you mean all the copies have gone?" Rosie asked the man behind the counter.

"We sold the last two copies to someone about an hour ago," he snapped. The village shop was brimming with noisy campers who were choosing treats for midnight feasts. The man was on his own, and a redness was creeping up his neck as he tried to serve everyone bundling up to the counter with their mixtures of sweets and handfuls of coins.

"But we've all been at Hillside," Mia frowned. "And why would someone buy two copies of the same magazine?"

"Do you remember what that person looked like?" Charlie called over, but the harassed shopkeeper had moved on from their conversation to serve the next camper.

The girls retreated from the bustle of the shop, and stood on the pavement outside in the hot sunshine.

"Great," Rosie said. "Our chief suspect suddenly seems innocent and we still haven't got hold of a copy of *Pony Mad*. So what now?"

"All we can do when we get back to camp," Charlie said, "is go over what we've got so far."

Mia pocketed the mints she'd bought for Wish, and felt something else in there. She pulled it out. It was the devil's claw sachet. With everything else that had been going on, the Pony Detectives hadn't even given this clue a second thought. Mia turned the sachet over in her hand. Suddenly the shop door pinged open behind her and the rest of the camp spilled out noisily onto the pavement.

As Mia quickly slipped the sachet back into her pocket, she wondered again why a rider would keep the devil's claw a secret. *It couldn't be linked to Foxy's disappearance,* she thought to herself. *Could it...?*

Chapter Ten

THE four girls headed straight to the paddocks to check on their ponies. In the next field, they saw Amber sitting near Copper, deep in thought.

"Are you feeling better?" Rosie called over.

Amber nodded. "Thanks for asking," she smiled back, looking much happier than when they'd left her at lunchtime. "I popped home to see Aunt Becca and helped with the animals."

"Any news on Foxy?" Rosie asked.

Amber shook her head. "Sorry I snapped earlier about the photo, Rosie. I wasn't feeling myself."

Their conversation was interrupted as Watty, closely followed by the rest of the blue team, ran noisily into the paddock, keen to tell Amber what she'd missed out on. Amber sighed.

"I'll have to catch up with you later," she said.

The Pony Detectives left Amber to it with a sympathetic shrug, knowing she'd probably be stuck with the blue team for ages. They caught a glimpse of Holly in the stables, chatting with Destiny, then they hurried inside their tent and went into a huddle.

Rosie chomped noisily on a cereal bar as Mia flipped her notebook open. She tapped the book with her pen, pointing to a couple of clues that she'd written down earlier in the week.

"Before we start, do we need a lookout?" Charlie asked.

"I can stay by the door," Alice offered. She got into position, then Mia began.

"Okay, so we all agree that finding *Pony Mad* in the muck heap, with part of the Lily Simpson article missing, suggests someone at camp knows something about Foxy's disappearance, right?"

"Right," the others nodded.

"At first everything pointed to Freddie," Mia continued, "but now it seems seriously unlikely that he's the culprit."

"So who does that leave us with?" Alice asked, chewing her lip. The Pony Detectives sat quietly for a moment, thinking hard.

"What about Holly?" Rosie asked, tentatively. The others looked at her, waiting for her to continue. "I mean, some of the things she's done don't quite add up – like her going missing on Sunday. She wasn't in the tent or the stables when she said she was."

"And she returned from wherever she'd been with chestnut hairs on her," Charlie added.

Mia nodded, her thick ponytail falling over her shoulder as she started to make notes.

"And Holly knew where my *Pony Mad* was," Rosie said. "She was late coming to our welcome talk on that first day – she could have taken it then!"

Alice lit up, forgetting to listen at the tent door as she thought of more clues. "And do you remember on that first hack Holly said she knew all the paths that led from Chestnut Grove."

"So?" Charlie frowned.

"So, she knows exactly where Chestnut Grove is, for a start," Alice explained.

"Maybe she knows all the paths," Rosie suggested, "because she's been hanging around there loads?"

Mia wrote the clues down, but didn't look convinced. "This does all look a bit odd, but it doesn't add up. Holly is Lily's biggest fan," she frowned. "There is no reason why she would want to steal Foxy."

The others sighed, knowing Mia was right – there was no reason.

Charlie read through the clues once more.

"Well, look," she said, "we haven't got anything else to go on, so maybe we should keep a closer eye on her for the next couple of days."

Suddenly they heard a tiny sneeze outside the tent. Charlie held up her hand and the Pony Detectives fell silent. They heard a light patter of footsteps moving away from them. Alice scrambled to the door and shoved her head through the flap. But when she looked out, there were lots of riders milling about. It was impossible to tell who, among them all, might have been listening.

υ υ υ υ

Once the ponies had fed and the haynets were hung up, everyone headed over to where the instructors were lighting a campfire, ready to cook sausages and veggie burgers to go with the mountain of salad that was waiting to one side.

As the light started to fade, the whole camp

sat around the fire on their sleeping bags and pillows. The flames and smoke snaked up into the inky sky, spitting and crackling. The instructors rubbed butter on the outside of potatoes, wrapped them in foil, then poked them into the ashes around the base of the campfire.

Melissa and Beth organised everyone into their teams. They handed out a pencil and sheet of paper with numbers down the side to each team. Holly went back to the tent to fetch her purple ink pen and notebook, so they could scribble notes if they needed to.

"Okay, guys, listen up!" Melissa called out over everyone's chatter. "It's time to start the quiz, so pens at the ready! Some of the questions will link into the stuff you've been taught in the last few days. Now we'll find out who's been listening!"

As everyone groaned jokingly, Freddie called out the first question.

"At shows, what are the colours of the

first- to sixth-place rosettes?"

"Dancer wouldn't know what a first-place rosette looked like!" Rosie joked and Alice giggled.

As the other teams discussed the answer in urgent, hushed whispers, Mia neatly wrote down the purple team's answer. Silence fell again, then the next question was asked.

"What are the principles of feeding?"

"For us or the ponies?" Rosie called out.

Mia rolled her eyes, as Charlie joined in the giggling with Alice. As Amber sat, racking her brains, Holly flipped open her notebook and quickly scribbled a few points down. She showed them to Mia who copied them silently from the purple-tinted paper.

"Next question," Beth said. "This is a picture round."

Melissa and Beth handed round pieces of paper with pictures of four different sets of horses' teeth drawn on each.

"You need to match each of those pictures with the ages I call out," Lara said, as the smell of burgers and sausages cooking began to drift across to where they were sitting. "One of those pictures is of a two-year-old's teeth, one is of a five-year-old's, one's an eight-year-old's and one's a sixteen-year-old's."

Before the rest of the purple team even got a chance to discuss it, Holly had written an age against each picture.

"Next question!" Melissa called out.

The questions came thick and fast about stable management and riding, including some technical ones about approaches to different cross-country fences, and skin conditions they'd been taught about. But yet again, before the others had even begun to think about the answers, Holly was already scribbling them down.

"There's no point doing this if you're going to take over," Amber muttered grumpily, sitting back on her sleeping bag and feigning disinterest.

Holly flushed pink and looked awkward. She kept quiet for the next question. It was about which essential nutrients a pony needed each day and none of the others knew the answer. Finally Holly bobbed forward and shyly listed them.

"That's awesome," Charlie said. "So, official rule – you're forbidden from being quiet from now on, Holly!"

Amber glared at Charlie. "We don't know if her answers are right yet, though," she pointed out.

Charlie frowned but didn't say anything more.

U U U U

When they'd finished, the teams all swapped sheets. Freddie read out the answers to a mixture of cheers and groans.

"I don't believe this!" Emily called out at

the end of the marking. "It must be a fix!"

"What?" Destiny asked, looking over.

"The purple team have got nearly *every single question* right," Watty said, as Beth began to collect the sheets and some of the teams got up and began to mill around. "They must've cheated."

"We're just lucky to have an equestrian super-brain on our team, that's all," Charlie grinned. "Holly."

"I wouldn't be surprised if she *had* cheated," Amber said, half under her breath but just loud enough for Holly to hear.

Holly looked upset. She stood up awkwardly, and moved to sit with Destiny and the rest of the red team on the other side of the camp fire.

Charlie tutted. "I don't understand why you're picking on Holly all the time," she said. "I thought you'd be happy that she knew the answers – it helps our team score, after all."

Amber rolled her eyes. "It isn't about the

team score," she said, "or anything to do with the stupid camp competition."

"Really?" Rosie said, sceptically.

"Oh, forget it," Amber said, getting up. "You probably wouldn't believe me if I told you, anyway." With that, she stormed off.

"Do you think we should go after her?" Mia asked.

"Um, can we do that *after* we've eaten?" Rosie asked.

The others agreed. They quickly shovelled in some food, then went to look for Amber.

They found her in the stables, sitting in the semi-dark with Copper. As they approached, she fished something out of her pocket and handed it to them.

"There, look at that," she said. Mia took the envelope that Amber was holding out. "Aunt Becca gave me this today. She said it was hand delivered last Sunday, the day after we started camp."

The writing on the envelope was in purple ink.

"Lily gets lots of fan mail and we all open it to help her out," Amber explained as Mia pulled a pale purple sheet with faint ponies down the side from the envelope and unfolded it. "Fans often want a signed photo, or an autograph, that kind of thing. This one stood out because it was written in purple, so I opened it … This is what I found."

Mia's heart started to thud as she read it out loud.

Dear Lily,

I'm your biggest fan — you're the best rider in the world and I'd love to meet you one day. You're my inspiration, and I want to get to Burghley just like you have. I don't live far from you. I'd love to help out at your yard, sweeping up or tidying the muck heap — anything. It's my dream to have a lesson with you — and I'd do anything to make that happen. Maybe one day!

I know you must get lots of letters all the time, but I hope you have time to read this one. I've got something I'd really like to show you — it's something I think you'd want to know about, and something you'd be really happy to see, too!

Please reply to me to find out about what I've got — who knows, you might think it's worth a lesson!

Your biggest fan,
Holly Benwell
xxx

"See?" Amber said, prodding the letter. "Everything you need's right here."

"Everything we need for what?" Charlie asked, confused, wondering if she'd missed something.

Amber rolled her eyes. "I thought you said

you were detectives. Here, read it again. Look – Holly would do *anything* to have a lesson with Lily, and she's got something that might be worth a lesson in return. I'm convinced Holly stole Foxy to get a lesson with my sister – if she finds him, Lily will be really grateful, and a lesson would be the least she could do to say thanks. But actually all Holly's done is wreck Lily's chances of becoming the youngest ever Burghley winner. *That's* why I'm off with Holly."

At that moment they heard Skylark whicker. They all turned to see Holly standing by his stable. She stroked his inquisitive big nose, as she looked over at the girls.

"Melissa's just rounding everyone up for bed," she told them. "Are you coming?"

"In a bit," Mia replied, guiltily wondering how much she'd overheard.

"Okay, well, I'll see you back there," Holly said. She lingered, looking between the Pony

Detectives and Amber. She gave Skylark one last kiss, then left the stables.

"What will you do about it?" Amber asked.

The Pony Detectives looked at each other.

"Did you say it was hand delivered on Sunday?" Rosie asked. Amber nodded. "That was the day Holly disappeared for ages. And came back with chestnut hairs all over her."

"I reckon we should tail her," Charlie suggested. "That way, if she does disappear from camp again, we'll find out exactly where she sneaks off to."

"And that might lead us straight to Foxy," Mia said, pocketing the letter.

They said goodnight to the ponies, then crept back into the tent, grabbed their wash bags and headed to the bathrooms. On the way back, Amber realised that she'd left her toothpaste behind, and said she'd catch the others up.

When the Pony Detectives ducked back into their tent, Holly was lying in her sleeping bag, her face to the canvas. Holly didn't move once, but Alice had a feeling that she wasn't asleep.

Chapter Eleven

"I can't believe it's got even hotter," Charlie said, sweltering in the heat as she finished mucking out the next morning. She put the wheelbarrow away and began to head for the Hall to get breakfast.

Mia, Rosie and Alice walked with her, already feeling sticky after morning stables.

"We're *definitely* going to melt in our body protectors," Rosie grumbled.

They walked into the dining room. Holly had been up and out of the tent before the Pony Detectives had woken, and she was already sitting with Destiny. She looked up when the girls walked in, and gave them a small, uncertain smile. Watty was in her usual position by the score sheet, shouting out the marks.

"Holly's even further ahead, by sixteen points now!" she announced. "Unless something disastrous happens, I don't think anyone can catch her!"

"Unless everyone gets inspired by Lily Simpson starting Burghley today," Emily added, winking at Amber. "Then there might be a gazillion points being scored!"

Amber studied the score sheet, then went to sit with Watty and her gang. They got into a conspiratorial huddle.

Mia looked back at the scores. Watty was right – there was nothing Amber could do now to claw back the lead from Holly. It looked like her ambition of winning first prize for the week was officially squashed.

Alice sat down with her cereal, and noticed that the murmuring in the hall was suddenly getting louder.

Destiny looked round. "Sounds like Watty's

getting a bit wound up at that end of the table, just for a change!"

Alice followed Destiny's gaze to see that the huddle had broken up.

"There's no way we'd do that," Watty said in a loud whisper, looking shocked. She got up. "Not even to meet your sister. Come on, blues, let's go."

The team marched out, leaving Amber sitting alone at her end of the table. A few seconds later, she got up too, and walked quickly out of the dining hall with her head down.

♘ ♘ ♘ ♘

Alice gave a nervous shiver as she scratched Scout's warm, damp, dappled neck. The purple team were out on the cross-country course. They'd walked, trotted and cantered their ponies, then Freddie had walked with them over to fence sixteen – the telegraph poles and hill. The riders had to jump one telegraph pole at the base of a small hill, canter or trot up the hill and through some flags at the top, then back down the hill and over another telegraph pole at the bottom. They'd warmed their ponies up by flowing over the bottom fence one after the other, and then the next – the shark's teeth – followed by the pheasant feeder. Now they were standing in line, facing a broad-topped jump with rolled edges.

"At fence twenty you've got two options," Freddie explained, slapping his hand on the flat top of the solid jump. "When you get to this point in the course you can either jump the smaller option just over there, called the hog's back, or you can take on this fence, the Joker. Anyone who decides to jump the Joker and clears it will get an extra twenty points."

Amber looked up sharply.

"But let's start with the hog's back," Freddie said, as Alice, Mia and Rosie let out a collective sigh of relief.

Alice gathered her reins and popped Scout into canter, following on behind Phantom, Copper and Skylark. Scout cantered confidently into the round-topped fence, adjusted his stride slightly, and flew over. Alice balanced on top, starting to feel less nervous. She turned after she'd slowed Scout to a trot to watch Wish jump elegantly, tucking her oiled hooves up neatly and looking picture perfect, if slightly slow. Rosie had got Dancer really fired up and she stormed up to the fence, and had a little look before ballooning over in a flurry of hooves.

"Okay, so who fancies tackling the Joker?" Freddie asked.

"Me and Phantom are up for a challenge," Charlie said, putting up her hand at once.

"I could probably go under it with Dancer," Rosie suggested.

Freddie grinned at Rosie, shaking his head. "Anyone else want to have a go?"

"Can I try with Skylark?" Holly asked Freddie.

He smiled, then nodded. "He can do it," Freddie said confidently.

Amber glanced over, then raised her own hand uncertainly.

"Are you sure?" Freddie asked.

Amber gulped, and nodded.

"Okay, well, let's see how we go," Freddie suggested. "Right, let's start with Phantom."

Freddie talked the riders through their approach. "This fence is much scarier for the riders to canter up to than it is for the horses," he explained. "You need to make sure you've got an energetic canter. Don't chase your pony into it, but don't let the canter get too slow either. And let him stretch over it, because of the width. Charlie, off you go."

Charlie took a deep breath and set Phantom going. He bounded into a forward canter, his slick ears flickering back uncertainly as he sensed Charlie's tingle of nerves.

"We can do this, Phantom," she whispered,

as much to herself as to him, and she turned and approached the table. It loomed up, broad and vast, and she held her breath. It didn't seem possible that they could reach the other side. But she kept her legs on Phantom's sides as he took his last stride and together they flew up and over the wide jump. It felt like they were suspended in the air for ages before Phantom stretched out his fine front legs and landed, to cheers from the watching riders.

Charlie cantered him back, catching her breath. "That was *huge*!"

Holly went next on Skylark. His big hooves marked a rhythmical beat on the grass. Holly's expression was one of pure focus. She set him up perfectly, so that he didn't get too deep or stand off too far. He sprung up boldly with a grunt, trying his hardest to reach for the far side. His hooves touched down again and the group gave another cheer, while Holly grinned from ear to ear, leaning down to hug Skylark.

Amber sat in the saddle looking pale.

"Are you sure you want to do this?" Freddie asked her gently.

"Course I am," Amber scoffed dismissively, but Mia noticed her hands shaking on the reins.

Amber pushed Copper into a fast canter. She circled wide, then turned towards the table. Copper began to take charge, his speed increasing towards the broad fence.

"Not too fast, Amber!" Freddie called out. "Turn Copper away if you're not in control!"

Amber was standing in her stirrups. She hauled on the right rein, and at the last moment steered Copper past the fence. The gelding's hooves skidded and he almost slipped over, but he just managed to right himself. When Amber finally managed to pull him up, she looked slightly sick. Copper jig-jogged back, anxiously fretting at his bit.

"If you're not one hundred per cent confident with a fence like this," Freddie said, walking over to reassure Copper with a pat, "it's best not to tackle it. It's a biggie to get wrong."

Amber bit her lip. "It's not that I wasn't confident," she explained quickly, "but Copper got his striding wrong and I didn't want to frighten him ahead of tomorrow. And, well, I think I'm just a bit nervous because Lily's about to start her dressage test at Burghley really soon! I can't concentrate."

Freddie looked unconvinced. "Well, okay, but I think you should still stick to the hog's back in the competition tomorrow."

Amber didn't reply, and as Holly glanced over at her she just looked the other way.

Freddie checked his watch then clapped his hands, suddenly snapping back into briskness. "Okay, that's it for today's lesson. The last fence – the tree trunk – is really straightforward, so you don't need to practise that one. Let's get the ponies back and turned out."

Everyone began to take their ponies back

on a long rein and Freddie quickly walked on ahead. He quickly disappeared into the Hall as the purple team gathered by the hoses near the carriage arch. They sloshed over with water buckets to give to their sweating ponies, who drank deeply. Charlie and Rosie hosed Phantom and Dancer, then ducked their own heads under the water themselves to cool down.

Once the ponies were hosed off, fly-sprayed and turned out in their paddocks, the girls rushed inside to grab a drink. They ran through the back door and heard the sound of the television drifting down the hallway. Grabbing a juice, they held the ice-cold glasses against their faces as they popped their heads into the lounge. The instructors were perched on the arm of a chair Freddie had moved up close to the television. They watched as Lily Simpson rode into the huge arena, elegant in top hat and tails, riding her awesomely big chestnut, Firestorm. More campers began to appear behind the Pony Detectives and they all edged into the room, standing silently by the sofas to watch the dressage test with their instructors. Amber hovered by Alice, her face a picture of anxious concentration and her eyes fixed on her sister. Lily finished with an immaculate halt and she saluted, then burst into a huge smile, leaning down to hug Firestorm.

Amber grinned back at the television, looking flooded with relief. The blue team congratulated Amber and patted her on the back as the next rider entered the arena. Freddie leaned closer to the screen. It was Georgie Belle's round.

He sat tensely, biting his nails, while Georgie performed her test. When she finished with a flourishing salute, he let out a whoop.

"Well ridden, Georgie!" he cheered. Over by the sofa, Watty giggled with Emily. Freddie cleared his throat, suddenly calming back down.

The girls watched a few more dressage tests, then grabbed their lunches and headed outside. They clambered over the post-and-rail fencing and plumped down under the shade of a chestnut tree with their ponies, watching as Watty and Emily dragged a couple of hay bales nearer the stables to have their lunch on. Alice shared her roll with Scout. A mixture of nerves about the competition and worries about finding Foxy swirled through her.

But she forgot her nerves completely when she glanced across and saw Holly. Alice had assumed that Holly was in the stables with Destiny, keeping Skylark and Topaz company on their no-grass diet. But instead, she was creeping round the edge of the cross-country course. To Alice, it looked like she was trying hard to not be seen.

"Quick!" Alice whispered urgently. "Holly's on the move!"

As the Pony Detectives got up and sneaked after her, Holly disappeared between the trees near the brook.

"Which way did she go?" Charlie asked as they sprinted onto the course as fast as they could.

Alice pointed, saving her breath.

They reached the lightly wooded area by the brook, and peered into the shady area. There was no sign of Holly.

"Well, let's just keep following the brook round," Mia suggested.

They kept jogging along, until they were totally puffed.

"At what point do we admit defeat?" Rosie gasped, as quietly as she could. At the same moment, Charlie saw a flash of purple T-shirt ahead in the woods, and warned Rosie to be quiet.

They kept low to the ground as they watched Holly jump down into the brook, splash across, and disappear on the other side. The girls waited for as long as they dared, then followed her.

"This is exactly where we rode through to

get to the lane on the treasure hunt!" Rosie whispered.

"If Holly knows this route, she must have taken it before!" Mia said as they splashed through the shallow brook. "And the furthest corner of Chestnut Grove's land is just the other side..."

They stayed under the cover of the trees as they saw Holly duck down through the hedge opposite and disappear. The Pony Detectives held their breath.

"That paddock belongs to Chestnut Grove!" Charlie gasped.

They tiptoed across the lane and stopped by the hedge. Alice pointed out the small gap near the bottom that Holly had gone through. They knelt down and peered through it. There, on the other side of the hedge, stood a chestnut pony under the shade of a large tree, near where the brook cut through the paddock.

"Hang on," Mia said with a frown. "That's

the paddock the old lady said wasn't used much."

"Well, it's being used now," Rosie said grimly.

Holly gave the pony a hug, then scrabbled through another hedge, leaving the boundary of Chestnut Grove's land.

"That explains the chestnut hairs," Mia whispered. The others nodded.

They watched silently as Holly ran across a small garden, up to the back door of the small, pale blue cottage. She rapped hard on the door. A few moments later, the old lady Mia, Rosie and Charlie had met during the treasure hunt opened it. She held out both her hands, breaking into a huge smile, then Holly stepped inside.

Mia quickly filled Alice in on who the old lady was, as Charlie and Rosie peered back through the hedge at the chestnut. After their initial excitement that it could be Foxy, their hopes were already starting to dwindle.

"That definitely does not look like a top eventing pony," Charlie frowned, running her eyes over the safe-looking small cob, "retired or not."

The girls sat back with a heavy sigh, but the next second they heard the cottage door opening again.

"Thanks for finding this, Grammy," they heard Holly call out, then the door closed.

"Grammy?!" Charlie whispered.

The four girls ducked across the lane and dived among the trees on the other side. They flung themselves down onto the grassy ground in time to see Holly run back across the lane and into the woods, carefully holding what looked like an old black-and-white photograph.

Chapter Twelve

"EVERYONE ready?" Melissa called out. She was standing in the heat with Freddie and the other instructors, waiting for the campers to get organised for the course walk.

The Pony Detectives had just gulped down ice-cold juices and now it was time to head out.

Holly had got back before them, and they found her spending the last ten minutes of lunchtime with Destiny inside the stables. Both girls gave their ponies one last big hug before stepping outside.

"I hate it that Skylark has to stay inside when it's so sunny out here," Holly sighed as she stood next to Freddie at the front of the group.

"I know," he agreed, "but it's better than if he eats lots of grass and gets laminitis."

"True," Holly said.

The last group of riders joined the waiting throng. Alice noticed that the blue team were carefully keeping their distance from Amber, for once. Holly, reaching into her pocket, walked timidly over to Amber, just as Melissa called out Amber's name.

"Amber, can you leave that glass behind please?" she said. "Cans and plastic bottles are okay."

"Sorry," Amber said, "I'll just tip it into a bottle. I've got one in my grooming kit. I'll catch you up."

As Amber stepped back inside the stables, Holly's face dropped.

Freddie clapped his hands and grinned. "Okay, let's go!"

Everyone headed out into the searing sun in shorts, vest-tops and flip-flops or deck shoes.

The Pony Detectives stuck together, with Alice getting more nervous with every step.

"I feel so sick!" she groaned.

"We haven't even got to the starter flags yet!" Rosie giggled as they approached the beginning of the course. Amber ran to catch them up, and they walked together in their big group, over the hill, round the slopes and down through the small copse of silver birch trees.

"It doesn't seem so bad on foot," Destiny said, "but this drop felt enormous looking down from Topaz's neck!"

"This whole course feels a lot longer on foot," Rosie said, wiping her damp forehead, "that's all *I* know. Poor Dancer – she has to carry me all the way round at canter!"

Alice noticed Holly keeping close to the instructors. She didn't have her notepad with her, but she was listening carefully to every word they uttered. She wasn't even distracted by the boys, who were messing about, leaping over the fences themselves and tripping up, or splashing through the water to cool down.

They all moved slowly round the course, talking about each fence in detail. They walked up to the brow of the hill towards the two flags they'd have to ride through the next day. Mia paused for a second at the top of the hill to check the line she'd ride on Wish. As she walked through the flags, she saw a flash of movement out of the corner of her eye. She glanced down the hill towards the paddocks and noticed Phantom and a few of the other ponies trotting round, their tails up. Mia frowned as they stopped, snorted and all stared in one direction. Wondering what had spooked them, Mia followed their gaze towards the stable block. She gasped as she saw smoke rising up and flames starting to lick the outside of the canvas.

"Fire!" She gulped, her heart almost jumping out of her chest, causing her words to get stuck in her throat. She got them out on the second attempt. "FIRE!"

The whole group ran as fast as they could down the other side of the hill to the stable block. The sun was fierce, and the slight breeze was fanning the flames, sending them flickering from one row of stables across to the next. Even as they ran, they could hear high-pitched, terrified whinnies.

"Skylark and Topaz!" Mia cried.

Holly pushed herself, running faster and faster, but it was Freddie who reached the paddock rails first and leaped over.

Alice felt fear rise in her throat as the other instructors stopped the rest of the campers at the paddock rails. Ahead of them, the ponies were careering around their fields, heads and tails raised. They were far enough from the rapidly spreading flames to be safe, but the desperate whinnies from inside the stables and the growing fire had sent them into blind panic.

"Everybody, I need you to follow me *around* the paddocks!" Melissa called out. "It's too dangerous to run through the ponies right now."

The campers immediately diverted their course and raced after Melissa – all apart from Holly. She flew into the paddocks, ignoring the danger, running as fast as she could. As Alice watched from a safe distance, she realised that Holly would have run straight into the burning stables, too, if Freddie hadn't grabbed hold of her.

"Let me go!" she screamed, trying to wrestle herself out of his grasp.

The rest of the campers came to a panicky, breathless halt by the tents. They were helpless. All they could do was watch in horror as the flames took hold, fiercely raging, spitting and popping in front of their eyes. A wall of heat kept them back.

Beth raced to the far end of the stables

and grabbed the hose. She directed the spurt of water right into the flames. Melissa had already rung the emergency services and Alice heard Freddie shout to Holly, "Go to the other campers – NOW!"

The next instant, Freddie took off his T-shirt, soaked it in the hose water, then covered his face with it.

"Freddie, don't!" Beth yelled.

But Freddie ran into the burning block. Behind him, Holly didn't go back to the campers. Melissa ran to get her, but Holly wouldn't budge and stayed, transfixed and shaking by the stables. Alice stood in the group, her eyes stinging. Seconds seemed like hours as everyone looked anxiously towards the flames, willing Freddie to reappear.

Suddenly he burst through the smoke at the tent end, coughing hard. Beside him was Topaz, Freddie's T-shirt over her eyes. She panicked, trying to shoot away sideways and kicking out. Freddie held onto her for all he was worth, until Lara rushed forward and slung the belt from her jodhpurs round Topaz's neck. Destiny rushed to open the nearest paddock gate. As Lara led her through it and removed the T-shirt, Topaz bolted forward, breaking free to join the herd.

Charlie stood frozen as Freddie faced the flames again. She watched, terrified, as he was beaten back by the heat, but he tried a second time. She saw Holly standing with her hands to her mouth as Freddie failed to get past the flames.

"Get out, Freddie!" Melissa yelled. "You'll be killed!"

Freddie still tried to battle forward into the acrid smoke. Charlie craned to see as he disappeared from view, but seconds later he reappeared.

"I'm so sorry, Holly," he gasped, coughing. "I... I can't get back in for Skylark."

"We *have* to!" Holly screamed, her eyes wide. "We... we *can't* leave him in there!"

She ducked past Freddie and tried to sprint in, but he caught her arm, swinging her back to him.

"It's too dangerous, Holly!" Freddie shouted.

For a second Holly fought to get free, but as part of the stabling collapsed and the fire took a fiercer hold, she stopped. Her face crumpled and she dropped to the floor, crying out in pain. All the campers watched her hopelessly, some of them in tears. Mia's insides twisted, as she imagined how she'd feel if it was Wish trapped in there.

Melissa rushed forward and helped Holly get to her feet, then supported her past the burning stables to the hall. Alice heard sirens sound in the distance, and minutes later she watched as a fire engine raced up the avenue and into the lorry park. She wanted to shout that they were too late. Firemen leaped out as the engine stopped, a co-ordinated unit unreeling thick hosepipes under the carriage arch.

As thick jets of water began to pump out of the pipes, the flames began to die back with a steamy hiss. Thick plumes of white smoke drifted upwards into the blue sky. Everyone turned away, horrified by the thought of Skylark trapped in there. Alice felt the tears choke in her throat, as she thought about Skylark leaping over the cross-country fences just hours earlier, bucking for joy, full of life. Holly would never hear Skylark's welcoming whicker ever again. Alice was unable to take it in.

As soon as it was safe, Beth quickly hurried the campers past the charred ruin, through the carriage arch and into the Hall. She led them to a large sitting room up the stairs, and told them to stay there until the fire was completely out.

The next hour seemed to last for ever. The ponies in the paddocks started to calm, although they wouldn't settle to eat. The firemen raked through the remaining ashes, and searched around the ruined framework. Freddie was out there too. He looked like he was in a daze.

"They're trying to find what caused the fire, I bet," one of the boys said, looking down from the first-floor window.

Charlie frowned as she looked over to the blue team, who were still keeping their distance from Amber. They kept glancing over at her as they whispered amongst themselves.

After a while, Amber left the room to get a drink. While she was out, Watty spoke quickly to the room. "Does anyone else think it's odd that we were just saying at breakfast that it would take a disaster to stop Holly winning the competition? Well, that's what we've had, and Amber was so desperate to be top of the leader board…"

Alice looked confused for a second. "Hang on," she said, "you can't think Amber started the fire on purpose?"

"Well, she was the last one in the stables," Emily chipped in. "She nipped back in just before our walk. Funny, don't you think?"

"And check *this* out," Watty added dramatically. "At breakfast she asked us to mess up Skylark's stable so that Holly would lose points in the inspection. She was *that* desperate to win."

The door opened and Amber walked back into the room. Watty and Emily stopped talking and looked away pointedly. Amber noticed and sat down heavily on her own once again.

"I know Amber wanted to win," Mia whispered to her friends, "but I don't think she'd actually start a fire, do you?"

Her three friends shook their heads.

After a while the door creaked open and Holly crept into the room. She came in with Melissa, and sat quietly by the window on the arm of a chair. Her eyes were puffy, her face still pale beneath her tear-stained, sooty cheeks.

The room fell quiet.

"We're all really sorry, Holly," Destiny said, rushing over. Her voice cracked.

The pain was etched on Holly's face. The tears began to tumble again at Destiny's words. She took a deep breath and wiped her eyes with a crumpled tissue. She nodded her thanks, then turned to look out at the blackened mess of stables, her forehead resting on the cool glass.

Beth came into the sitting room and had a quiet word with Melissa, then disappeared again.

"Okay," said Melissa. "The rest of the instructors will be back in a while, then we'll have a camp meeting."

There was a general murmuring as people wondered what was going to be said.

Destiny was called back out when a vet arrived to check on the horses. Topaz was ordered home to rest after inhaling smoke. In the long hour that followed, Destiny's mum arrived with a trailer. Destiny left with Topaz and her mum, promising to return once her pony had settled.

The Pony Detectives carried on looking out of the window. One of the firemen was crouching near the end of the burned-out stables. He lifted something and showed it to Freddie, then he walked the instructors through the remains of the structure.

They stopped by Skylark's stable. Nothing was left but an empty shell, the grass around it charred. The fireman explained something to the instructors, who listened intently. Then Freddie raked his hands through his hair. He turned and began to walk away, then broke into a jog to his battered Land Rover. He jumped in, started the engine with a roar and flew off through the carriage arch, past the stable ruin and the tents, then onto the estate land.

"I bet he can't bear to hear about Skylark,"

Rosie said. "His mum said that he chose him, remember? He must be as crushed as Holly."

The afternoon dragged on. Then, all of a sudden, Holly stiffened in her seat by the window. Everyone turned to look as she stood, slowly, her hands spread out on the glass. Her breath was still, her eyes fixed on a point in the distance – beyond the carriage arch, the stables and tents, through to the pastureland.

Her lips moved but she whispered so quietly no one could hear her.

"What did you say?" Mia asked, trying to follow Holly's fixed gaze.

Then Holly whispered again. "Skylark!"

In an instant everyone fell silent. They peered out of the window and there, walking along the brow of the hill like a ghost, was the grey pony, his feathery hooves stepping high.

Next to his noble, roman-nosed head, walked Freddie.

"How...?" Charlie gasped, as everyone else quickly rushed to the open window. Holly pushed back through them, running to the stairs. They watched as she burst from the back door. She sprinted through the carriage arch, around the charred remains of the stables and through the tents.

As she ran, she called out to Skylark. Alice saw Skylark prick his ears at the sound of Holly's voice. Then they heard his welcoming whicker. Freddie let go of him and the grey pony broke into a jog, then a canter. Skylark careered towards Holly and the two of them skidded to a halt together. Holly jumped up, throwing her arms around the pony's thick neck, burying her face against it. Skylark stood stock still, and for a moment they stood locked together on the grassy slope.

Chapter Thirteen

"So, was Skylark in the stables when they caught fire, then?" asked Destiny. She had just been dropped back at camp and had joined everyone in the reception room. The amazement of seeing Skylark, as if somehow he'd risen, phoenix-like, from the deadly flames, had stunned them all.

"The firemen reckon he must have kicked his door open in a panic, and escaped before the fire really took hold," Beth explained.

"Is he okay?" Charlie asked.

"The vet's out there now with Holly and Freddie," Melissa said. "They're worried about his hooves. Freddie found him down near the barns, by the path that leads to Hilltop. If he's been out for a while, he may have had a chance to settle and graze on all the rich grass down there."

"So even though he escaped the fire," Rosie sighed, "he might end up with laminitis."

"He must've been trying to get home," Charlie said.

The next moment the door opened and Freddie and Holly stepped in. Holly looked in shock, like she couldn't quite believe what was happening around her. The campers immediately rushed over to her, asking how Skylark was doing.

"Let's have some quiet for a moment, please!" Melissa called out over the noise. The conversations died down.

The instructors stood near the television. Melissa nodded at them, as if she was checking something, then began to speak. Melissa asked the campers how they felt, and everyone talked for a while about how scared they'd been.

"Do the firemen know what started the fire?"

one of the boys from the green team asked.

Freddie shook his head. "Not yet," he said. "They're still looking into that."

Alice noticed Watty and Emily exchange a look, then glance at Amber.

"Can we go out and check on our ponies?" Charlie asked. "I really, really want to see Phantom."

"I can't wait to see Dancer, either," Rosie chipped in, as everyone else started to say they wanted to see their ponies, too.

"We've checked all the ponies in the fields," Freddie reassured the campers, "and they're all okay."

There was an audible sigh of relief around the room.

"What's going to happen to them tonight now the stables have gone?" Mia asked.

"They'll have to stay out overnight," Melissa explained, "if you all still want to stay for the end of the camp. How does everyone feel?

Do you want to stay? Or would you rather go home now?"

Everyone turned to each other, checking with their friends next to them.

"I'd like to stay," Mia said to her three friends.

"Me too," Alice agreed as Charlie and Rosie nodded.

Around them the rest of the campers were saying the same.

"Okay, well, that's brilliant," Melissa said, looking round to check everyone agreed. "So, now we want to discuss something with you all about the competition. It's amazing that both Skylark and Topaz have survived today, but neither of them will be able to take part in the cross-country tomorrow. So, given that they would lose out on the points from that activity, how does everyone feel about the cross-country – should we cancel it? If we do, the competition results will stand as they are as of today."

"We can't cancel it!" Amber blurted out. Most of the campers turned and glared at her.

"Maybe Holly and Destiny should decide," Mia suggested.

"Good idea," Melissa agreed.

"What do you think, Holly?" Destiny asked uncertainly.

Holly twiddled the bit of tissue she was holding in her hand. "I guess... I guess it should go ahead," she said, glancing at Amber. "I mean, it's what everyone's been training for."

Destiny nodded in agreement.

"But what about the scores?" Charlie pointed out. "You're in the lead, Holly. It's not fair if you can't compete, then get beaten."

Holly half smiled. "I can't stop everyone competing just so I stay in the lead."

"Holly wouldn't," Watty whispered loudly, "but I wonder if someone else in this room would stoop that low?"

Amber glanced up and turned slightly pink.

"Can I go and see Copper now?" she asked, suddenly looking desperate for an excuse to leave the room as everyone's eyes turned on her.

"Just a sec, Amber," Melissa said. "So we're agreed then, campers. The cross-country competition tomorrow goes ahead. Now, off you go and see your ponies."

Everyone left the room and headed around the soaked, blackened outline of the stables to the paddocks. Phantom was still spooked, and Charlie couldn't get near him or Hettie. But she could see by the way he floated around the field that he was okay. Dancer trotted over to Rosie, stopping abruptly as she bumped into her. The unsettled pony's eyes were still goggly. As Rosie gave her a reassuring pat, Dancer took the opportunity to rummage for a treat. She shuffled an apple out of Rosie's pocket and greedily scrumped it from the floor. Wish and Scout had already calmed down and were grazing. They walked over to see Mia and Alice, looking for some fuss.

As Alice stood with Scout, she looked across the fields to the other ponies. Copper paced the paddock, unsettled like Phantom. Amber was sitting on the fence, kicking her heels against it. She looked over as Freddie, Melissa and Lara built a small area with electric fencing around the poorest grass, for Skylark to be turned out in. Then she turned with a sigh back to Copper.

Scout nudged Alice to get her attention, then turned it into a general rub of his forehead against her arm. She'd just given him almost half her packet of strong mints when she heard Melissa calling out that it was time to feed the ponies.

The evening conversations while everyone carried feed buckets to the paddocks and then had their own dinner were full of Skylark and Topaz's dramatic escapes. After they'd eaten,

Holly and Destiny went to check on Skylark while the others collected their cross-country start times for the next day. The red team, without Destiny, would be out on the course first, followed by the green team and then the purple team, minus Holly. Last to go would be the blue team. The start times were pinned up by the score sheet. Alice saw Amber move from the time sheet to the score sheet.

"See you back in the tent," she said quietly to the Pony Detectives, as Watty and Emily looked over with a bit of a scowl.

Alice studied the score sheet, too, before she headed back to the tents with the rest of the Pony Detectives.

"Amber could still win," she said to the others, "now that Holly's out of the competition. But she'll have to jump the Joker to get enough points to do it."

Rosie shivered. "No prize would make me want to tackle that."

"And judging by her attempt earlier," Charlie said, "Amber would be pretty silly if she tried it on Copper tomorrow."

"I bet you anything she does, though," Mia said.

When they reached the tent, Amber was already in there, lying quietly on her sleeping bag, her face to the tent wall. Holly joined them a few minutes later, covered in white hair.

"How's Skylark?" Rosie asked. "Is he settled?"

Holly nodded.

Once everyone was in the tent, Amber sat up and rummaged through her bag.

"I've left my phone somewhere, I think," she said, quietly. "I've been carrying it around in case Lily or Mum call about how things have gone today. I must've put it down somewhere. I better go and find it."

Amber slipped out of the tent. Alice frowned. Every night Amber had misplaced something vital, and she'd had to go back out of the tent after lights out to find it. At first it had seemed forgetful, now Alice was starting to wonder if there was more to it. While the Pony Detectives got changed for bed, Holly flipped open her notebook. She scanned through all the notes she'd made about the cross-country course.

"That'll still be useful one day," Mia smiled, looking over. Then she noticed something about the notepad. She reached into her suitcase and found the letter that Amber had given them to read, then carefully opened it, out of sight, beside her camp bed. She glanced back at Holly's notebook. The paper was the same – both sheets had pale horseshoes printed down one side. But in the notebook there was an image of a horse across the top of the page, too. That image was missing from the letter, as if the top of the letter had been cut off.

As Holly shut her notepad and put it down, an old black-and-white photo slipped out. It was of a huge, raw-boned horse with a small lady rider in the saddle.

"Wow," Mia said, impressed. "Who's that?"

Holly picked up the photo and studied it for a second. "Meet Flame Thrower," she said, glancing up quickly, then back at the photo. "And that's Grammy in the saddle."

Holly fell silent, aware of everyone looking over at her.

Charlie leaned closer to get a better view of the photo. "How come you brought this with you?" Charlie asked.

"Oh, it's a bit of a long story," Holly said, looking uncertain. The Pony Detectives nodded encouragingly, eager to hear more.

Holly smiled. "This picture was taken at Chestnut Grove, ages ago. Grammy used to work there when she was young. It was a stud back then and she helped deliver Flame as a foal. After a few years handling him, she broke Flame in and did all his early training. He was sold to someone called Captain Stobbard and they won Burghley together. Apparently, the captain always said that it was Grammy's hard work that made Flame Thrower such a brilliant horse. When the Captain retired Flame, he sent him back to Grammy. She still worked at Chestnut Grove at that point, so that's where Flame lived for the rest of his life."

Holly stared at the photo and took a deep breath before continuing. "When he died, at twenty-seven years old, he was buried near a big chestnut tree in the furthest paddock. Soon afterwards, Grammy retired too, and moved into a little blue cottage, just the other side of the paddock. She couldn't bear to be parted from Flame. She's lived there for years and years now. I visit her every spare second I get – I love hearing all her stories about the old horses she used to foal and break in. She's got photos and old rosettes everywhere, and bits of old tack. It's nothing like my house. Mum and Dad are complete neat freaks – they get stressed if my dirty riding boots clutter up the hallway. Anyway, I thought Lily would like to see this picture. I thought that if she knew a chestnut horse from her yard had been trained to win Burghley years ago, it might inspire her to win even more."

"So, did you get to show it to her?" Alice asked.

Holly shook her head, and cringed slightly, sheepishly looking round at the girls. "I wrote to her when she first moved here, at the beginning of the school summer holidays. I said I had something important to tell her. I never heard back anything though, even though I wrote my address at the top. I wrote the date and 'Welcome to our village!' in different coloured felt tips to try and make it stand out. The other day I wondered if Amber might like to see the photo. I know we're not meant to leave camp, but I sneaked out to ask Grammy if I could borrow it. She dug it out for me yesterday, just before the course walk. I hoped if I showed it to Amber, it... it might make her like me. It was the only thing I could think of."

Mia's mind began to race. She needed to talk to the other Pony Detectives alone. One thing was clear – the letter that Amber had shown them had been trimmed down, so that they hadn't been able to tell when it had been written. Holly had told them she'd sent the letter at the start of the summer holidays – over a month ago – but Amber had said it had been delivered at the start of the week. And that could only be for one reason, Mia thought as her heart thumped: to put Holly squarely in the frame for Foxy's disappearance.

Suddenly a phone let out a neigh, buzzing with an incoming text, making everyone jump.

"That's Amber's," Rosie frowned. "But I thought she'd gone out to look for it?"

Charlie leaned over Amber's camp bed. Her wash bag was tucked down by the side, and her phone was sitting just inside it. As she looked, Charlie caught sight of some small rectangular sachets, shoved into a side pocket of the bag. They looked familiar. She pulled one out. The words 'Devil's Claw' were emblazoned on the front. Suddenly the tent door zinged open. Charlie dropped the sachet like it was on fire and hastily jumped back off Amber's camp bed.

"Found my phone," Amber said as she stepped back inside. She looked round at the sea of faces, and frowned as she sat down on her sleeping bag. Then she froze for a second. Charlie realised that she must not have put the devil's claw packet back in the right part of Amber's wash bag. And Amber must have realised that the whole tent had worked out she'd lied about her phone.

But Amber didn't say anything. She just chucked a T-shirt over her wash bag and silently climbed into bed.

Chapter Fourteen

FROM the moment they climbed out of their tents the next morning, everyone was rushing round like crazy, getting ready for the cross-country competition. There were no stables to muck out, but the ponies had to be groomed to perfection, and their tack polished.

The Pony Detectives hardly had a minute to themselves to catch up from the night before, but over breakfast they managed to huddle together at the end of one table.

"So, Holly can't have had anything to do with Foxy's disappearance," Charlie whispered, "not now her letter to Lily's been explained."

"But I don't get why Amber would try to frame Holly," Alice said.

"Or why she'd be wandering about with devil's claw in her wash bag," Charlie added.

"Unless..." Mia said, her eyebrows pinching together, "unless she's feeding it to one of the ponies here?"

Rosie gasped. "What if Amber's been sneaking off to the feed room every night?" she whispered. "It would have been the perfect opportunity to add it into one of the feeds without anyone seeing her. They'd be made up ready for breakfast."

Alice noticed Amber look over at the four of them. Her pale eyebrows furrowed as she stood up and carried her plate over to the side. Alice saw that her hands were shaking.

"Come on, everyone," Melissa said, as the instructors stood up to leave the hall, "time to start tacking up!"

"Well, there's not much we can do right this second," Charlie said to the others in frustration. They still had no clue where Foxy was, and they were rapidly running out of time left at camp to find him – the holiday was nearly over and they'd be going home the next day. "We'll have to wait until after the cross-country now."

They headed outside. The ponies, sleek coats shining in the early morning sunshine, were tied to the paddock fences as their riders buzzed about. Holly and Destiny were both outside, helping the riders by fetching water buckets and sponges or sprinting to the hall to fetch ice-cold drinks.

"Okay, first team ready?" Melissa called out, as the reds made last-minute adjustments to their tack. They jumped on board, then rode over to the warm-up area.

Once they were ready, riders would set off every three minutes. The blue team started to tack up, getting their ponies' boots and saddles on. They left the bridles hanging on the paddock rails next to them. The ponies stood, their eyes half closed, one back leg resting. Their tails casually swished the flies away and they shook their heads, stomping a front hoof.

Copper was restless, not standing still for a second as Amber tried to groom him. As Amber returned from the tack room, carrying her own saddle and bridle for once, Charlie made a face.

"He looks like he might be handful today," Charlie said.

Amber gave a weak smile. "I know," she replied. "I'm going to get on him in a second so I've got loads of time to warm him up before we start. Then hopefully I can get some of the fizz out of him." She pulled on her riding gloves and clicked her body protector into place, then glanced round at the riders bustling to and fro. "Oh, by the way, I bumped into Holly and Destiny near the tack room. Holly said she had something to tell you. I think she was heading into the feed room."

"What, now?" Alice asked, glancing over to

Scout and wondering how much time they had before they were due to mount.

Amber nodded.

"We'd better be quick, then," Charlie said, starting off in the direction of the feed room. The others followed and stepped out of the sunshine into the cool shade. They'd just got inside when they heard footsteps approaching.

Alice was about to look and see who it was when the door suddenly swung shut in her face. Before she could react, the big key was turned in the rusty lock. She tried the handle, rattling it desperately. The door shook, but wouldn't open.

"Someone's locked us in!" she cried as Charlie rushed over and started to bang on the door. "We're trapped!"

"It's no good," Mia said. "No one will hear us from the paddocks – they're all gearing up for their cross-country starts."

"If this is one of the boys having a laugh,

I swear I'll bury them in the muck heap!" Charlie said, banging the door again crossly.

"Somehow, I don't think it is them," Mia said, staying calm. "But whoever it is, we need to find a way out of here, quick."

"Well, maybe there's a spare key somewhere," Alice suggested, looking round at all the tins on the shelf. "We'd better get searching."

While Alice and Mia checked the shelves, Charlie and Rosie searched around the feed bins.

"There's something under here," Rosie puffed. She grabbed a wooden mixing spoon and poked around.

"Is it key-shaped?" Alice asked hopefully, moving onto the next shelf.

"I can't tell yet," Rosie grunted, trying to reach further under with the spoon. "I've nearly got it... oh!"

Rosie gave a final flick with her spoon and a copy of *Pony Mad* skidded out from underneath the bin, bringing with it a collection of screwed-up sachets. Alice grabbed one of the sachets, and flattened it out. "Devil's claw," she said grimly as Rosie ducked back down and fished under the bin again.

"There's something else caught under here," Rosie said, before a second magazine came sliding out. "Another *Pony Mad*! That makes two copies – these must be the ones from the shop!"

As Rosie flipped open the pages, looking for the article on Lily Simpson, Alice frowned. "But no one from camp could have bought them. We were all at Hilltop when the shop sold out."

"Apart from Amber," Mia suddenly remembered. "She said she went to see her aunt, but she could easily have nipped into the village too. And these were under the feed bin in the same hiding place as the empty sachets. It has to be her!"

"She knew everyone wanted copies of *Pony Mad* from the village," Rosie said, "so there's got to be something in this magazine article on Lily that she didn't want any of us to see."

"Yes, but what?" Charlie asked, impatiently.

Rosie turned the pages, almost ripping them in her haste.

"Hang on, here's the fact file on Lily's top horses and ponies," Rosie said, skimming through the article. "Foxy… here we go… So, he's sixteen, he loves his chin being rubbed and he has one devil's claw sachet in his morning feed. It helps keep him pain free after retiring through injury two years ago!"

"Well, I guess that explains how Amber managed to get a stash of it," Alice said, "she must have taken it from Chestnut Grove."

Rosie suddenly gasped. "Look! There's a picture of Copper in the magazine!" The others quickly looked over her shoulder.

"But the caption says it's Foxy, not Copper."

Mia frowned, double-checking. "They must have got it wrong."

They all stared at the picture of a pony with the same white blaze as Copper, spread slightly over one eye, and an identical pink patch on his muzzle. The only difference was that the pony in the picture looked roughed off. His mane was longer and fluffier, and he had whiskers under his chin. But it still looked just like Copper.

"And look," Alice pointed out, "it says there that Foxy's the only pony on the yard with a freeze mark. But Copper's got one too, hasn't he?"

Mia's heart raced as fast as her mind. "If that's right, then all this information can only mean one thing... Copper must be Foxy!" she gasped. "Amber was so desperate to win that she sneaked one of Lily's top ponies into camp and tried to pass him off as her own!"

"That means Foxy's been here, right under our

noses, all along," Rosie said, shaking her head.

The Pony Detectives looked at each other, amazed by Amber's reckless plan.

"So where, then, has Amber hidden the *real* Copper?" Alice added.

"How did she ever think she'd get away with swapping ponies like this?" Charlie asked.

"And why would she go to such lengths," Mia said, still feeling stunned as Rosie carried on reading the article, "just to win a Pony Camp competition?"

"Oh my goodness," Rosie whispered, her heart starting to race. "If that is Foxy out there with Amber, he's in serious danger. Listen to this! Fact number seven: Foxy retired through injury. He damaged the ligaments and tendons in his near fore. He's come back into work, but he can't do anything too strenuous because if he injures his leg again, his tendons could be damaged beyond repair. The injury would then be life-threatening!"

"But Amber's about to jump him round a whole cross-country course! *And* she's planning to take on the Joker! I can't believe she'd be willing to risk Foxy's life, just to get to the top of the leader board!" Alice cried. "We've got to get out there now! We have to stop her!"

All the time Rosie had been reading out loud, Charlie had been searching the feed room. She'd been about to give up when she suddenly had an idea. She quickly grabbed a broken whip from the bucket in the corner, tugged off the flappy end bit, then prodded the exposed fibreglass shaft into the key hole.

"Er, what are you doing?" Rosie asked, frowning.

"Trying to get us out of here," Charlie puffed. With a clink, the key dropped to the ground outside. Charlie quickly lay on her tummy on the ground, then slid the broken whip through the gap under the door. She scooped the whip, carefully teasing the key towards her.

"Bingo!" Charlie cried, as it slid through the gap. "Let's go!"

She grabbed the key, turned it in the lock and the four girls fell out into the sunshine. As they raced to the paddocks, they looked over to the start of the cross-country course.

"Where's Amber?" Charlie called over to Holly, who was standing next to Phantom, a concerned look on her face.

"Never mind Amber, where have you four been?" she asked. "It's nearly your turn on the course! Me and Destiny have been looking everywhere for you!"

"You could have tried the feed room!" Rosie cried. "Just tell us, has Amber gone out onto the course yet?"

"She started a few minutes ago. She'll probably be nearly at the end by now." Holly frowned. "Why?"

But the girls didn't stop to explain. They grabbed their bridles, quickly put them on their ponies and leaped into their saddles.

"Sorry, Phantom," Charlie said to her horse, who skittered sideways as she shoved her feet into the stirrups. "But we've got to fly!"

The four girls cantered their ponies past the tents and out onto the estate grounds. As they reached the end of the trees that lined the paddocks, Amber and Foxy galloped into view. They were in the distance, but the girls could see that Foxy was flying up to the steps, his tail spread like a banner behind him, and every muscle under his copper-coloured coat was taut.

Amber was standing up in the stirrups, trying to steady him, but it was clear that she'd lost control of the chestnut gelding. He skidded coming into the first step, suddenly realising what was in front of him. He bunched up and scrambled over the first couple of steps. Amber was unbalanced, but somehow she managed to cling on. Foxy took one big stride on the top then bounded down the drop. Amber almost tipped over the front. With all the weight over his shoulders, Foxy stumbled as he moved away from the fence and for the next few strides his steps faltered.

On top, Amber looked pale and grim, but determined. She pointed her gutsy pony at the tiger trap and flew over, and was quickly onto the telegraph poles. They sailed over that combination and the shark's teeth, too, but when Amber tried to turn him towards the pheasant feeder, Foxy started to prop, putting in short strides and raising his head. He spun round once, trying to edge towards the trees that lined the brook around the boundary.

"He's trying to get back home to Chestnut Grove!" Mia said as they pushed their ponies on.

But Amber wouldn't let him. She raised her stick and gave the little gelding a half-hearted slap on his rump. Foxy leaped forward, shocked. His stride got faster, his head up. Amber tangled her fingers into his mane with one hand as she yanked on the rein with the other, turning the recklessly galloping pony towards the pheasant feeder. They flew over. As Foxy's speed got even faster, Amber hauled on the reins to turn the pony towards the Joker fence.

"Amber!" Charlie shouted. "Don't jump!"

Melissa was jump-judging and she looked over to the Pony Detectives, then to the out-of-control pony. She immediately got on her radio.

Amber was locked on the fence. Foxy's head was high and he only saw it in the last few moments, suddenly adjusting his stride and launching himself into the air. He scrabbled over it in a muddle of hooves before landing awkwardly on the other side. He stumbled onto one knee, and looked like he was about to fall, but somehow he righted himself just in time. But Amber was shot out of the saddle and, free of her, Foxy suddenly turned and began to bolt back to the brook.

"He'll end up on the lane!" Mia called out. "Quick!"

The gelding's strides were uneven. His reins tangled round one leg as he raced on in a blind panic. The Pony Detectives squeezed their ponies into a fast canter, and set off in pursuit, flying past the table, the pheasant feeder and the shark's teeth. The trees weren't densely packed and the girls could see Foxy splash down into the brook, then spring out the other side. They had just ducked into the woods after him, sliding with their ponies into the brook when they heard it. A clatter of hooves on the lane and a squeal of tyres. A sickening thud followed, then silence.

"Foxy!" Alice screamed.

They clambered out of the brook, their hearts pounding, then scrambled out of their saddles and walked their ponies through the trees on the other side.

"I don't want to look," Rosie whispered, as they emerged onto the lane.

There in front of them, scrambling up from the road, stood Foxy. Alice saw ugly grazes all down his near side, blood beading rapidly from each one. There was a deep gash on his hip, stifle and hock. Foxy was trembling all over, his head low, his breathing laboured. He attempted to move, then clearly thought better of it. He swayed, then stood stock still.

Charlie grabbed hold of Wish's reins. Mia wanted to rush forward, but she made herself step quietly up to Foxy, before gently taking his bridle. Rosie chucked Dancer's reins to Alice and quickly undid Foxy's scuffed girth and slid off his saddle.

Further up the road, a car had come off the road and come to a halt. The driver climbed out, shakily, as the door to the blue cottage was flung open.

"It's Holly's Grammy," Alice whispered.

The old lady was very sprightly for her age. She ran to the road, her face full of concern, and helped the driver over to the wall to sit down and recover.

Melissa splashed through the brook and emerged onto the lane. She already had her mobile phone glued to her ear, and within seconds the girls realised she was on the phone to the vet. She acknowledged the Pony Detectives with a nod, then took in Foxy's injuries and the dented car with a sweep of her eyes.

"Yup, it's bad," she said, catching her breath. "Fifteen minutes? Okay, I'll organise a trailer."

She radioed through to Freddie and the girls heard him say that he'd get a trailer from Hilltop.

Melissa spoke to the driver to understand exactly where Foxy had been hit, so that she could tell the vet.

"He came out of nowhere," the driver kept saying. "The pony came out of nowhere. I... I couldn't avoid him. Will he be okay?"

Melissa avoided answering the driver's

question as Amber appeared behind them, a grass stain on her hip from where she'd hit the ground. She froze, taking in Foxy's drooping head, the dark sweat on his neck, his heaving flanks and the blood pouring from where he'd hit the tarmac. And he was pointing his near foreleg, not wanting to put weight on it.

"Amber, what were you thinking?" Charlie demanded, shaking with anger at the sight of Foxy.

Amber didn't respond. She just stood there, staring at Foxy and barely breathing. "That's the leg he injured before." She spoke in an almost inaudible whisper. "What have I done?"

Charlie's anger drained away at once as she saw the guilt and fear on Amber's pale face. She leaned against Phantom, who for once stood stock still.

Melissa looked between the four friends and Amber. "Would someone mind telling me what on earth is going on?" she demanded. "What do

264

you mean by the leg Copper damaged before? There wasn't anything on his form to say he had an injury."

"This isn't Copper," Mia said.

Amber stayed silent for a second, then looked up at the pony in front of her. "No, this... this is Foxy."

"What, Foxy as in your sister's retired eventer, Foxy?" Melissa asked, confused. Then it sunk in. "You mean you had him at camp all this time?"

Amber nodded, her eyes fixed on the ground. Melissa looked stunned. As they waited for Freddie to arrive with the trailer and the vet, Amber stood, pale-faced and with tears streaming silently down her cheeks. She moved over to Foxy and rubbed under his chin, but the gelding didn't respond. His eyes were wide and staring as Amber whispered to him, stroking his ear over and over.

Suddenly a car appeared, slowed to a stop,

and a tall, broad woman in overalls jumped out. Alice felt a flood of relief wash over her – it was the vet.

The vet examined Foxy, checking his eyes and heart rate as Melissa explained what had happened as best she could.

"He's in shock on top of everything else," the vet said, giving him an antibiotic injection into his jugular vein, and another into his hind quarters. Foxy staggered slightly, looking confused all of a sudden. "He needs fluids, fast. We'll have to take him back to the surgery for that. Trailer's on its way, I take it?"

At that moment, Freddie appeared, roaring round the corner. Within minutes they'd lowered the ramp right in front of Foxy, and helped him to move stiffly into the trailer.

"Okay," the vet said, checking her paperwork, "just to confirm, this is Copper, right?"

"No, it's Foxy," Melissa said.

The vet crossed something out on her sheet

266

and scribbled the new name. Freddie, standing with them, gave a start.

"Sorry, did I hear that right?" He looked from Melissa to Amber, who nodded miserably.

"Yes," Amber whispered.

Freddie stared at her, taking it in for a second. "But Lily's been going crazy about Foxy all week! She's hardly been able to concentrate at all!" he said, getting cross. "How could you be so thoughtless, Amber?"

Amber hung her head for a second, then she looked up with a puzzled expression. "How come you know so much about it?"

"Georgie may be Lily's biggest rival," Freddie said, "but despite all that the media say, they're also close friends. Both of them nearly withdrew from Burghley so they could come back to search for Foxy. I've helped Georgie train so hard… Getting her to Burghley has been our plan for ages and she nearly threw it all away to help her friend out. I had to promise that

I'd keep a lookout from here, just to persuade her to stay. Didn't you stop to think what taking Foxy might do to Lily and everyone around her?"

Amber stood miserably, looking down at the ground once more.

Freddie reached for his phone. "I've got to let Georgie know. She can tell Lily that Foxy's been found."

"No!" Amber pleaded, desperately. "Please don't tell Lily! At least, not yet!"

Freddie frowned. "She has to be told what's happened, Amber."

"But she'll rush home as soon as you call her!" Amber cried, glancing at Foxy. "And I... I've ruined enough for her already without completely wrecking her chances at Burghley, too."

He put his phone away. "All right. But I'm going to ring Georgie as soon as I know more about what's happening." With that he jumped into the Land Rover and drove away steadily, following the vet.

As the trailer disappeared, Rosie noticed the old chestnut pony they'd spotted during the treasure hunt. He was poking his face through the hedge, trying to see what was going on. Amber saw him, too. Her eyes filled up again as Melissa came over.

"Can you four take Amber back to camp while I make sure the driver's okay?" Melissa asked.

They nodded, then silently splashed their way in single file through the brook. Amber trailed behind them, her eyes fixed firmly on the ground.

Chapter Fifteen

THE Pony Detectives led their ponies back, the water soaking into their jodhpur boots. Amber stayed silent. After they were back amongst the cross-country fences on the estate land, she glanced up at the girls, then looked back at the ground.

"I... I didn't mean to hurt Foxy, you know," she said quietly.

"Funny way of going about it," Rosie sniffed, not feeling much in the mood for forgiveness after seeing the terrible state Foxy had been in.

"Forget it, then," Amber said, tears of frustration welling up. "I knew you wouldn't get it. No one ever does."

"Get what?" Alice asked, shooting Rosie

a look. Rosie rolled her eyes, but kept quiet.

Amber sighed heavily. "How difficult it is being Lily Simpson's sister, that's what."

Charlie frowned. "What's so difficult about that? Most people would think you're the luckiest person in the world!"

"What's lucky about having your whole life turned upside down because your mum thinks your sister's ambitions should come above everything else?" Amber asked, her pent-up desperation suddenly spilling out. "I've left everything behind – friends, school, my home – all for Lily's dream. Everyone I meet over here is only interested in me because I'm Lily Simpson's sister. And she's amazing at everything she touches. I've lived my whole life in her shadow, second best in everything. And here, at camp, for just one week I wanted to be the best.

"I wanted to go with them to Burghley, but Mum thought I'd get in the way, so she booked me in at camp. I was meant to be bringing my reliable old pony Copper. Mum and Lily left on the Friday and I... I just had a mad five seconds on Saturday morning and decided to swap Copper for Foxy. Lily had pulled his mane and trimmed his tail when she brought him back into work, so he was good to go."

"But you said he was roughed off!" Charlie gasped.

Amber looked embarrassed. "That was just to put you off the trail, that's all. He had been roughed off, up until a few months ago. Anyway, I left Copper turned out in the corner paddock. He had plenty of fresh water from the brook, and there's lots of grass for him in that field."

"Was that him," Alice asked, "in that field back there?"

Amber nodded miserably. "I thought I could borrow Foxy for the week, win the competition and return him before Lily got back. I thought she'd never have to know. I even rode Foxy here the back way, taking him through the brook and round the edge of the estate. I led him through a paddock by some barns, which brought us out on tothe track next to the hall. That way we kept off the lanes and out of the way of Aunt Becca, who drove to Dovecote Hall to drop my stuff off."

"So that explains the chestnut hairs on the gatepost by the barns…" Charlie said, glancing at the others.

"I thought I'd got away with it," Amber continued with a sniff, "but then Lily called home. She'd forgotten to tell Aunt Becca about feeding Foxy his supplement."

"The devil's claw?" Rosie asked.

Amber nodded. "Aunt Becca asked Lily how she could identify Foxy amongst all the ponies. Lily said it was easy – he's the only pony with a freeze mark. None of the ponies had rugs on, so it didn't take long for Aunt Becca to check them all. When she did, there wasn't a freeze mark in sight. Lily wanted to come back at once – but if she had, my plan would have been ruined. So when she decided to stay, I thought I was home and dry. Only, then I discovered that Foxy wasn't easy to ride at all. I thought he'd be a cinch, because Lily had won so much with him. But with me in the saddle he just got stronger and stronger. By then I was trapped – I couldn't tell anyone that he was too much for me without confessing to what I'd done."

"And to top it all, you came up against Holly," Mia sighed, starting to understand that being a famous rider's sister might not be as great as it sounded.

Amber nodded. "Holly's such a naturally gifted rider, and everyone was heaping praise on her," she said. "I was second best again. It was like having Lily here at camp with me. I couldn't help it, but I began to hate Holly."

Amber was silent for a moment, wiping her nose. The she looked up earnestly at the four girls beside her. "I know I've been an idiot, but I never set out to hurt Foxy and I honestly didn't start that fire," she said. "I'd never do that."

"No, we didn't think anyone would do that on purpose," Charlie said.

Amber looked relieved. "I couldn't believe it when you said that you had a copy of *Pony Mad*. I had to hide it – I knew that once you'd seen the photo of Foxy you'd figure out what I'd done straight away. I took it out of the tent when I had the phone call from Lily – it was the perfect opportunity to get rid of it while everyone was in the dining room. I thought you'd given up on your search, but you hadn't. I overheard you talking about it again, during the week. You had a couple of clues that could put Holly in the frame, so I went home and dug out the letter she'd sent. I wanted to put you off my trail. But last night I realised I'd got a text while I was out pretending to look for my phone. I figured that you'd probably seen the devil's claw sachets, too. You were getting closer to rumbling me. But I'd dug myself in so deep by that point that I just had to keep going. I tried to get Watty to help me. I thought she'd do anything to meet Lily. But it turned out that even she's got some principles, so she said no. Then I had to win the stupid competition, just to make it all worthwhile."

Amber hung her head. The tears started to flow again. "I've messed up so badly, and I've been so mean to Foxy, and Copper, as well as Lily and Holly. I don't know what to do, or how to say sorry to everyone."

The girls were silent for a second. "Well, you'll just have to hope that the vets can help Foxy," Alice suggested. "But there is *one* thing that might make it up to Holly." As they walked back together, Alice told Amber her idea.

As they reached camp, they were suddenly surrounded as everyone swarmed forward, wanting to know what was happening. Amber stayed quiet while Mia gave a shortened version of what happened, without spilling the beans about Amber's lies. Amber looked over and gave her a small, grateful smile.

Once the Pony Detectives had convinced Beth that they were fine to ride around the course, the instructor clapped her hands, getting everyone's attention.

"Well, if everyone's okay, it looks like we can carry on with the cross-country competition," Beth announced. As the other campers cheered, the Pony Detectives smiled. They had to put Amber's revelations and their worry for Foxy behind them for a moment, in order to focus on the course ahead.

Beth carried on. "I've drafted in some extra jump judges from Hilltop, so we won't be short. Right, let's get going!"

There was a flurry of activity, and suddenly Charlie was out on the course. She warmed Phantom up, then headed out over the log pile. Phantom was keen beneath her, pulling slightly at the reins as he floated over fence after fence, making nothing of them. Her horse was fast, sleek and put daylight between his hooves and each solid fence, even the Joker. For the time that she was on the course, Phantom and jumping were all Charlie thought about.

Alice set out behind her, with Rosie and Mia by her side. They'd asked if they could ride together, and share any points. Melissa had agreed and suddenly the remaining riders had asked the same.

Mia finally let Wish stride on and the little mare flew. And, after all the training during the week and with Scout's tail to follow, Dancer finally excelled. She charged round, head down, like a tank. Rosie whooped, managing to clear everything first time from canter, apart from the steps, which Dancer goggled at like she'd never seen them before. But Rosie was determined and got her up them second time, earning a cheer from Beth, who was jump-judging there. They cantered on over the pheasant feeder, and opted for the hog's back rather than the Joker, then finished off over the tree trunk in fine style.

Rosie and Dancer both puffed through the finish flags, but Rosie had never felt more elated.

Holly helped them all untack and hose down their steaming ponies, fetching buckets of water which they drank gratefully.

Amber stayed slightly apart, still subdued, as everyone else stood and cheered the final riders back, one by one or in pairs. Watty shrieked through the finishing flags, having missed half the fences on the ill-tempered Ace.

When everyone had completed the course, the Land Rover and trailer rattled back up the tree-lined avenue and into the lorry park.

A few moments later, Freddie walked over to the paddocks.

"Amber," he said quietly, "could I have a word?"

♡ ♡ ♡ ♡

As the last ponies were settled back in their paddocks, Amber and Freddie emerged from the Hall. Amber smiled up at him. She still looked pale, but it was like a weight had been lifted from her.

Freddie joined the instructors, and they decided to have the prizegiving under the shady tree in Foxy's empty paddock. As the riders gathered there, excitedly chattering about the cross-country course, the Pony Detectives fell into step with Amber.

"Any news on the patient?" Mia asked.

Amber nodded. "There was a stone wedged in his hoof – that's what was making him go lame in front – and the grazes are deep but not life-threatening. He's recovering from the shock, too," Amber explained in a shaky voice. "The vet thinks he's going to be okay. Freddie called Georgie, and told her what had happened. She broke the news to Lily for me, then Freddie put me on the phone and helped me explain everything."

Tears welled up in her eyes again, but she hastily wiped them away.

Everyone fell silent as Melissa cleared her throat and addressed them all.

"I want to congratulate everyone who has contributed to Pony Camp. This year has been one of the most dramatic in the camp's history, but hopefully you've all had fun and learned lots too. And the first thing I want to let you all know is that the firemen have been in touch this morning. They found that there was nothing suspicious about the fire starting. Lots of campers ate lunch outside the stables, sitting on the hay bales. Someone must have rushed off for the course walk and left a glass on one of the bales by mistake. The sun was really intense, and the glass concentrated the sun's rays into one hot spot on the canvas. The firemen think that's what started the fire. No one is to blame, it was just a terrible accident."

Alice noticed Watty and her gang were squirming at having wrongly accused Amber.

"Now, to the prizes!"

Melissa began to hand out the prizes for individuals and the teams. Charlie won the red rosette and the trophy in the individuals, but she chose not to accept it.

"If Holly had competed today," she said, "she'd have won it, so it's only fair that it still goes to her."

Holly flushed pink as Mia, Rosie and Alice whooped and encouraged her up. Holly tried to protest, but Destiny persuaded her to go, and she collected the trophy and rosette.

"This is the first rosette I've ever won!" she said shyly, admiring it.

Charlie graciously accepted a blue second-place rosette, to a huge cheer from everyone. Alice was delighted with her fifth place and Mia with her sixth, which put the purple team in first place. The red team came second, helped by Destiny, who came third individually.

Once all the rosettes had been handed out, everyone began to talk again, until Melissa called them back to order.

"There are still a couple of rosettes left," Mia noticed.

"We have a special achievement award for the most improved rider and pony this week," Melissa announced and everyone began to murmur. "And I'm delighted to say that this goes to Rosie and Dancer!"

Rosie almost fell over, even though she was sitting down. When she did manage to get up, she did a little bow.

"Just go up there and get it!" Charlie said, shaking her head and laughing.

Everyone else giggled, shoving Rosie to the front.

"Now, our very last prize," Melissa continued, "is a very special one. It's for a lesson with Lily Simpson, as organised by Amber."

The whole camp gasped and began to look round, nudging each other and whispering about who would win it.

"And it's for the rider who has worked the hardest, and who showed the most natural talent this week." Melissa smiled, picking up another special rosette. "And, to prove that dreams can come true, Holly, this is for you."

Holly gasped, her eyes wide. "No way!"

"Yes way," Amber laughed.

"Oh, but hang on, I don't have my own pony..." Holly's face suddenly dropped.

Freddie smiled. "If you accept my offer

of taking Skylark on loan, you will. He's too talented to stay in the riding school. I'd love to train you both."

Holly's hands suddenly shot to her mouth. "Are you being serious?" She began to laugh and hiccup, all at the same time, like she couldn't believe what was happening. "I can't wait to tell Grammy!"

Lots of the campers congratulated Holly, and then raced down to the pool for a final evening swim.

"I can't believe this is happening." Holly giggled with Amber, Destiny and the Pony Detectives as she walked back to the stables to tell Skylark the good news. They all spent some time making a fuss of Skylark, before jumping in the pool.

That night it took ages for the camp to settle into silence. Everyone had decided to sleep outside under the stars for their last night.

"I'm going to miss this tomorrow," Rosie

yawned in the darkness as she lay down on her sleeping bag.

"Me too," Alice said. "And seeing the ponies all day, every day – and at night if we want to, as well."

"I'm not going to miss Rosie's snoring," Charlie laughed. Rosie flung her pillow at Charlie, who got out of the way so quickly, it hit Mia on the head instead.

"Rosie!" Mia squealed, getting her own pillow and thwacking her back.

"Time for sleep everyone," Freddie called out.

They lay back down giggling, before drifting off to the sound of the ponies snorting gently in their paddocks.

Chapter Sixteen

THE next morning, all the campers were flying round in a mad rush as everyone started to get ready to leave, flinging clothes into bags and dashing between tents to get everyone's email addresses, promising to keep in touch and taking crazy photos.

They'd just had time to groom their ponies and round up all their tack when the first of the horseboxes arrived. One after the other began to bump up the drive after that, and it wasn't long before Charlie's dad appeared. The four girls got their ponies booted and rugged up, ready to travel.

As Watty set off for home on Ace, she promised to drop by and call for Amber on a hack sometime soon. Suddenly Watty wanted to be best friends again. Amber rolled her eyes.

When Watty had gone, Holly led Skylark over to Amber to say goodbye.

"I can't wait for your lesson at Chestnut Grove," Amber smiled. "Or to meet your Grammy properly and find out more about the place. I told Lily about your photograph. She remembered your letter and said she was going to reply once she'd got settled in. She's really excited now she knows more of what you wanted to tell her about."

Holly grinned. "I'm so excited about it, as well! You'll have to come to mine, too. We can watch horsey DVDs!"

"Hmm, I'm going to rethink my horsey future after this week," Amber joked. "Maybe it's time I started to learn a musical instrument instead!"

Holly grinned, then set off with Skylark back to Hilltop Riding School. Her parents were meeting her and Freddie there to talk through his plans for her future riding career.

As Alice got ready to lead Scout from the field, she looked round, feeling sad that it was suddenly all over.

"I wish that we didn't have to leave either," Charlie said as she saw Alice's face. "Though the sooner we get back, the sooner we can get the ponies settled down. And the sooner we can sit down to watch Burghley cross-country! The holiday hasn't ended just yet!"

"We'd better get going then," Rosie said, leading Dancer towards the horsebox.

∪ ∪ ∪ ∪

With the ponies all loaded, the girls were just about to head off when Amber ran up to them. She gave them a Foxy update – he'd be coming home in another couple of days, and was recovering well.

"Apparently he's being the model patient. Oh, and thanks for yesterday," she said, looking a bit awkward for a second. "For waiting with me in the lane and, well, for listening to me. After what I'd been like all week I was pretty amazed that anyone would speak to me, so it meant a lot. And I want to buy you a replacement copy of *Pony Mad*, Rosie, to make up for taking yours. I'll send it to you in the post, if I take your address."

"You don't have to worry about doing that," Rosie said.

"I was going to get Lily to sign it for you all," Amber explained.

"Ooh, well, scratch what I just said," Rosie smiled. "You do have to worry about doing that! Thanks, Amber!"

Mia wrote down the Blackberry Farm address and Amber wrote down hers, too.

"If you are ever around," she said, shyly, "I'd love it if you could pop in. You could meet Lily, too."

They all grinned. "We will," Mia said. "But it doesn't matter if Lily's there or not. It'd just be nice to catch up with you."

Amber smiled warmly, just as her Aunt Becca arrived to collect her. Aunt Becca did not look very happy.

"Right, we'd better leave you to it," Charlie said, knowing that Amber had some explaining to do. "Good luck!"

The girls jumped into their horsebox and waved a last goodbye to Pony Camp.

⋃ ⋃ ⋃ ⋃

"And there's just one more fence between Lily Simpson and the chance to make history at Burghley," the commentator said in a hushed voice.

The arena was so silent that each hoof beat could be heard clearly.

The Pony Detectives were sitting on the

carpet in Rosie's front room, watching the television. They'd done the same the day before when they'd got home from camp. They'd got the ponies settled, then sat glued to the screen, watching the horses fly round the massive Burghley cross-country fences. Rosie had her special achievement rosette attached to her T-shirt and Beanie, her Jack Russell, was lounging on her lap, rolling over to be tickled.

The others had giggled at Beanie, but all the joking around had stopped the instant Lily Simpson had appeared. They'd watched, captivated, as she and Firestorm jumped as one over the enormous brushes, ditches and the water complexes. The pair had gone round clear, and were sitting in first place going into the show-jumping phase on the final day of the competition.

Now the girls could barely watch as they counted down her strides to the final show jump – it was all that stood between her and a place in the history books.

"And she's done it! She's cleared the last fence!" the commentator screamed over the deafening roar from the crowd. "Lily Simpson has become the youngest ever rider to lift the Burghley trophy!"

The girls leaped up and danced round the room, whooping and high-fiving. They collapsed back onto the squishy sofas just as Lily was interviewed. She was crying and laughing at the same time, holding onto Firestorm with loose reins as everyone walking past hugged her or congratulated her. She talked about how thrilled she was and how amazingly lucky she was to have a horse like Firestorm. When asked who she wanted to dedicate the win to, she didn't hesitate.

"First, to my little sis, Amber," Lily said, looking directly into the camera. "I know she'll be at home watching. She's given up loads to come to the UK with me. I hadn't realised till this week just how hard it's been for her, and I hope this makes up for it just a little bit!"

"Sounds like Lily's forgiven Amber," Mia said.

Lily continued, "I want to dedicate this victory to the most wonderful pony ever, Foxy, who helped me get where I am today. He means the world to me and I want to say a huge thanks to everyone at Dovecote Hall Pony Camp who rallied round to help find Foxy when we thought he'd gone missing. You know who you are – thanks, guys!"

The Pony Detectives looked at each other like they might burst, and erupted into cheers.

"She meant us!" Charlie giggled. "I can't believe *Lily Simpson* thanked *us*!"

"On live television!" Rosie added, hiccupping through excitement.

"Our first celebrity case successfully solved!" Mia beamed. "Tick!"

They watched as Firestorm received a huge wreath round his neck, and tried to eat it.

"Just think," Charlie grinned, "one day that'll be Holly up there, winning Burghley."

"And we can say we know her!" Alice giggled.

"Er, aren't you forgetting another talent that might soon be charging round there?" Rosie said.

"Why, who else is there?" Charlie frowned. Alice and Mia tried to think who she meant.

Rosie pointed to the rosette pinned to her T-shirt. "Er, you don't get a special achievement for nothing," she said. "This year, Pony Camp – next year, Burghley! There's no stopping me and Dancer now!"

The Pony Detectives collapsed into another fit of giggles. As they settled back down to watch the trophy presentation, the four best friends grinned at each other. They were already looking forward to next summer, when they could go to camp all over again.

Turn over for some
fantastic pony tips from
The Pony Detectives and
their pals!

Pack For Camp With the Pony Detectives!

For you:
- ↻ Riding hat
- ↻ Body protector
- ↻ Jodhpurs
- ↻ Jodhpur boots
- ↻ Any show gear you may need
- ↻ Whip

For your pony:
- ↻ All your tack
- ↻ Buckets
- ↻ Haynets
- ↻ Feed
- ↻ Grooming kit
- ↻ Fly spray
- ↻ Shampoo
- ↻ Headcollar & lead rope

ROSIE'S TIP: don't forget some treats for midnight feasts!

How to be a
Cross-country Star

Follow Charlie's tips to become
a cross-country champ!

U Aim to get your pony into a good
rhythm right at the start of the course.

U Try to keep out of the saddle in the
cross-country position between fences. It
might make your legs ache afterwards, but it's
more comfy for your pony over a long distance.

U Prepare your pony for the fence ahead
by changing his speed on the approach. He'll
need to pick up speed to clear a spread, or
steady up for a tricky drop or bounce!

U Remember to keep the red flags on the
fences to the right, and the white flags to the
left when you jump a cross-country fence.

If your or your pony aren't confident about riding
in a cross-country competition, you could enter a
'pairs' class, where you ride round with a friend.

Dovecote Hall
Cross-Country Course

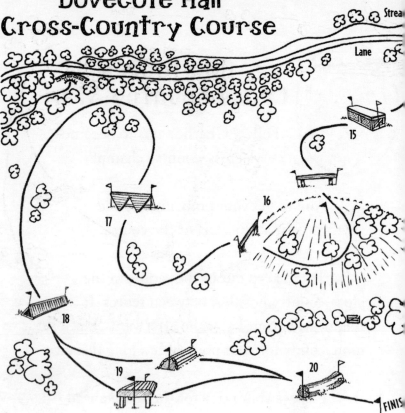

Stream

Lane

15

16

17

18

19

20

FINISH

START

The Jumps

1. log pile	8. hedge	15. tiger trap
2. tree trunk	9. water complex	16. telegraph
3. brush fence	10. trakener	17. shark's teeth
4. hayrack	11. tyres	18. pheasant feeder
5. sloping rails	12. log pile	19. hog's back
6. stone wall	13. tyres	or table (Joker)
7. bullfinch	14. steps	20. tree trunk

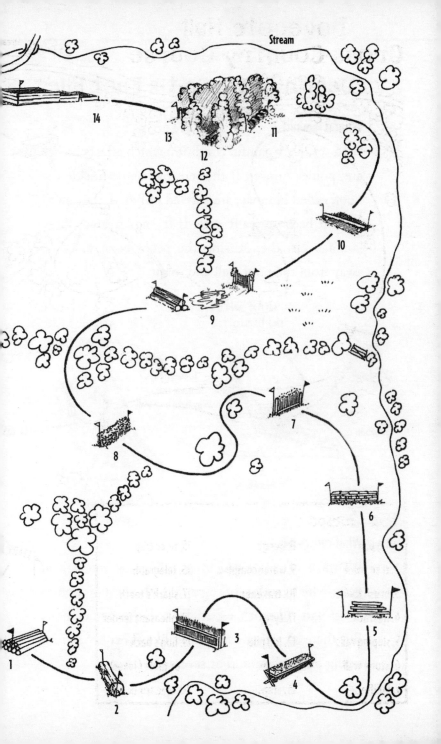

Stream

Destiny's Laminitis Fact File

What is laminitis?

It's a seriously painful condition which affects horses and ponies' hooves. If the sensitive tissues inside the hoof, called laminae, are starved of blood, they swell up and become really sore. If it's not treated, these laminae can die, causing the pedal bone to come away from the hoof wall and rotate.

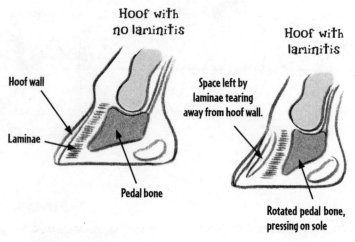

Hoof with
no laminitis

Hoof with
laminitis

Hoof wall

Laminae

Space left by
laminae tearing
away from hoof wall.

Pedal bone

Rotated pedal bone,
pressing on sole

What causes it?

It's most often caused by guzzling too much lush grass, which has lots of sugar in it. Overweight ponies are at particular risk, especially if they become obese. But there are other causes, too, like concussion from riding on hard ground or severe infection.

What are the symptoms?

A pony with laminitis may sit back onto his hind feet. He's likely to have heat in his front hooves, and he may not want to put weight on them. Your pony's hooves will have rings around them if he's had laminitis in the past.

How can you prevent it?
Keep a close eye on your pony's diet. If he's prone to laminitis, restrict his access to lush grass and keep him fit, so he doesn't become overweight. But make sure that you don't starve him. Every pony needs to eat little and often to keep his gut happy.

DESTINY'S TOP TIP:
Always call your vet if you think your pony has laminitis.